I0775455

ANGEL: BROKEN

ALSO BY S. N. MONTOYA

Angel

Angel: Broken

A Sequel to Angel

S. N. Montoya

First Edition, 2023

ISBN-979-8-9886040-3-7

EireneBros Publishing LLC

4414 82nd St, Ste 212, -318 Lubbock, TX 79424

www.eirenebrospublishing.com

www.facebook.com/EireneBrosPublishing/

Dedicated to the Montoya family, for inviting me into their home in which the entirety of this book was written. I am blessed to be able to share in their family name.

Prologue

"Angel!" Midnight cried, watching helplessly as Lucifer carried her away. *This is not how it was supposed to happen.* She thinks to herself. The prophecy was so clear. Angel kills Lucifer. She should have been full of rage when Justin died, not sorrowful. She blamed herself for his death rather than realizing the real cause was her enemy from the beginning.

Midnight moves her attention to Justin, who is lying heartbreakingly still. *She tried so hard to heal him.* She closes her eyes for a moment, taking a deep breath. *This can't be for nothing.* She refused to believe that the hope of winning was just ripped away. The girl she spent all that time training and encouraging…taken away from her.

"Midnight? What should we do?" Orion approaches her slowly, tears swelling in his eyes. She turns to him. The boy that had never fought a day in his life was standing before her now. Alive and well, covered in the blood of Lucifer's minions. Him being the only one to live feels ironic. *He needs to stay alive.*

"Leave." Orion jerks his head up, opening his mouth in protest. "Go back to hiding; we can't afford to lose another today. I will come back for you to discuss our next plan." She commands him with an authoritative tone.

"Fine, just make sure to come to me again." He lowers his voice, immediately breaking off into a run. *At least one of them is safe.* Midnight thinks to herself, happy to have him away from this mess.

She sits quietly for a moment, taking in the scene around her. The air is full of thick smoke, fiery ash floating around her. A multitude of dead dragons lay around her, their bodies slowly turning into black clouds. In seconds, all that remains of them is blood-stained snow.

Close to where Lucifer had snatched up Angel, Justin's body still lay completely still. *He can't stay here.* She tells herself, pushing the aching feeling away. She has a task to do.

She moves over to him, unable to take her eyes off his chest. She had watched Angel tear into him, yet underneath the blood…he looked untouched. She shifts her gaze to his neck, only to see that, too, is completely healed. *Impossible.*

Midnight immediately presses her ear against his heart, a hopeful feeling rising within her. *Nothing.* She rises back up, letting out a quick breath. *Shapeshifters can't heal. Besides, he was already dead.* She reminds herself. Even if Angel had somehow healed him, he was long gone.

Midnight continues with her task, trying to shake the dark feeling away. She gently pulls at the sheath wrapped around his waist; she will need it to cover the sword so she can carry it. It doesn't budge. Annoyed, she gives it a hard yank, shifting his body slightly.

A gasp escapes his mouth, causing Midnight to jump back in sheer panic. *That's impossible.* She watches in horror as his body jolts up, his hands clasping his throat as he takes a few ragged breaths. Their panicked gazes meet each other momentarily; Midnight doesn't say a word, noticing a green shimmer swirling around the brown in his eyes. *What on Earth?*

"Where is she?" He suddenly blurts out, his voice hoarse, jumping to his feet quickly, the movement causing him to stagger slightly.

"You were…you were…" Midnight stutters, watching as he frantically scans the area around them, horror filling his face.

"Where is she, Midnight!" He is yelling now, tears streaming down his face. She stays silent, the words caught in her throat. He stops moving for a moment, scanning her. *Don't make me tell you. I can't handle this.* She closes her eyes, letting her body droop slightly as she sighs.

"No, you said it yourself…you said that she was the chosen

one…she wasn't supposed to die." Midnight stays still as he grieves, trying to block out his choking sobs. The sound of the sword clattering fills her ears. He must have kicked it. *Why didn't I tell them about the prophecy? Not telling them made things so much worse.* She scolds herself. *If they had known, it wouldn't have happened. You know that.*

"Everything happens for a reason…We just don't know the reason for this yet." She whispers once his shouting has calmed down.

"It doesn't make sense…you said she was prophesized about. Is there any written evidence? A rune or something? You must tell me where it is." He meets her gaze with a fire in his eyes; all the grief drained from him.

"There were a few, but I am certain they are destroyed."

"Where?"

"Justin, you just came back from the dead. Give yourself a break before you go on some impossible quest." Midnight tries to keep her strength.

"Where, Midnight?"

"I am not going to tell you. Go home. This isn't your concern anymore." Midnight says coldly, trying to make him let it go. Even if he manages to find the prophecy, only shapeshifters can enter, and there is no way she is going back there again.

"Fine." He snaps, taking a deep breath. "I'll find it myself."

After watching him storm off into the forest, Midnight cautiously uses one paw to hold the sheath of the sword still while she slides it into place. She gently picks the entire thing up in her jaws and moves toward the woods. She couldn't trust keeping it in the cave right now, as Lucifer would surely come looking for it…after he finished whatever plan he had with Angel's corpse.

Before long, she gets the strange feeling that someone is watching her. She immediately stops in her tracks, scanning the dense trees around her for signs of movement. "Show yourself." She snaps, letting the sword fall by her feet.

Snow crunches in front of her as a figure moves closer. She narrows her eyes, noticing a rather tall woman with a surprisingly familiar face. *Arkadia?* She questions.

"What happened? What in God's name was that massive shock-wave, Midnight?" Arkadia stops directly in front of her, her eyes shifting to the sword. "And why are you carrying that in plain sight? Did you not feel Lucifer's presence?" She crosses her arms, trying to show her authority. *How can this day get any more surprising?*

"You're supposed to be dead."

Chapter One

Chaos

"You're not done yet." An unfamiliar voice echoes, pushing Angel's soul toward a portal with His own hands.

* * *

It was a strange place, full of newness and destruction. I was surrounded by darkness, completely unaware of who I was. My mind felt blank, fuzziness clouding it. A pair of pure white eyes stared at me from across the darkness, seeming to look into my very soul. I felt frozen as I stared back, unable to move. *What are you?* I ask myself.

A strange force suddenly pushes me toward the pair of eyes calling to me. Compelled by the force, I slowly reach out to the figure, my hands trembling. A soft yet firm hand suddenly grasps mine, pulling me through a tunnel.

My body goes numb as I go through, tingles surging throughout me. I gasp as I fall to my knees, feeling coming back to me.

I catch my breath. *Am I dead?* I think to myself, staring at the hard ground underneath me. The stranger offers her hand again, her now light green eyes meeting mine. She looked so different now; she was a shadow, but now a tall girl covered in shining metal armor stood before me.

"What is this place?" I ask her, trying to get a good look at my surroundings. Nothing seemed right. *I don't belong here.* I tell myself. This place feels much different than the dark abyss; I feel light, as though I am not truly here.

"This is the World of Chaos. I wasn't supposed to look at you, but I couldn't help myself. You are from Earth, correct?" She asks me.

"Earth, that sounds right. But… I am not sure. I…" I struggle to remember, a fiery sensation filling my head as I think. "I don't know; I must have lost my memory."

"And your wings, what of those? You're not an angel, are you? A demon, perhaps?" She questions, staring intently at the wings attached to my back. *I have wings?* I ask myself, completely in shock.

I let myself feel for them, stretching them out for a clearer view. They are white, and every feather has a black tip, making them appear slightly checkered. They are relatively large, the very tips nearly scraping the ground below. I twist my body around, stretching and turning them to understand how they feel.

Their bases are incredibly muscular; it is clear they were well-exercised. The feathers themselves felt delicate yet strong. They are full of nerves; I can feel almost every individual feather. Strange energy was surging through them, fueling me with strength and power.

"I didn't realize I had them. They feel strong; I must have used them a great deal." I say to her, continuing to admire their strength and beauty. "How come you don't have wings?" I add, curious as to why I was the only one.

She lets out a soft chuckle. "Wings are rare. Only certain people have them. But perhaps I can help you; this is a dangerous land - one that you should not be in for very long. I am Lana, by the way."

"It is nice to meet you, but I am unsure how you can help me remember. My mind is full of fire. Everything is so fuzzy in here. I don't even know my name." I reply, trying to sift through my head.

"I won't be able to, but I know someone who can." She says confidently.

"Why would you want to help me?" I ask her.

"I don't really know, to be honest. But something inside me is telling me to. I think we are connected somehow. Besides, I am the one that accidentally brought you here."

"Well, you did pull me out of a… Well, I don't know what." I say, turning toward the strange maze of mirrors. Her hand quickly turns my head away. "Wha—" I blurt out, surprised by the sudden contact.

"Don't look at them. You'll just pull more things through. Now, let me take you to my husband. He will be able to help. I am sure of it." *Pull more things through?* I question myself, shuddering at the thought.

"Is he far?" I ask her, my attention turning toward the vast and barren landscape before us.

"Not at all." She replies, starting to walk away from the maze.

A tall man comes into view. A mask covers his face, and he seems surrounded by darkness; the sight of him sends a shiver down my spine. He is evil, and my body is sure to let me know. He does not seem pleased to see us coming his way, his irritated eyes meeting Lana's. As we approach, my body pings with anxiety, begging me to run away.

"What have you done? She is not supposed to be here." He growls, making me take a few steps behind her.

"I couldn't help myself; she was calling to me. I think we are meant to help her. She is lost." Lana places a hand on me, pushing me in front so the man can see me clearly. *This is the last place I should be. Whoever you are that brought me here, send me back!* I shout in my head, desperately hoping they somehow hear.

"She is a dream walker," he says rather confidently, slowly approaching my side, taking small steps around me as he looks me up and down. *Is he studying me?* "She is nearly dead, but she is trapped. There is darkness of her own in her, fueled by regret and rage. She must remember who she was; otherwise, she may never be able to escape." I swallow hard, not moving a muscle as he touches my wing. He gently runs a hand through my feathers, making them tingle at his touch. Lana stands beside us, carefully watching him.

"Is she an angel or a demon? I cannot tell." Lana asks him.

"Neither, but she is a God's creation, a weapon of some kind. She's dangerous, Lana; we must be careful. Since she is a dream walker, she can't be harmed here. Not without mana." *Am I a weapon? A creation? What does this all mean?* I think to myself, running my hands through my hair. His eyes meet mine instantly, narrowing as he stares intently. I freeze up in an instant.

"I can try to reach into her with my darkness and untangle her thoughts." He suggests, continuing to stare into my eyes. "That is if that is what you want." I try to look away from his penetrating gaze but seem to be stuck in a frozen state.

"I…I don't know what I want, do as you wish." I whisper to him, barely able to speak. There is just something about him, his dark eyes and evil aroma. *Is he a demon?* I question. *What even is a demon?*

"Once I enter your mind and tap into your memories, you will be able to see them as well. You'll see what I see."

"Okay," I reply, closing my eyes to prepare myself. His hands touch my shoulders, causing my body to flinch slightly. Within a second, I feel his dark aroma engulf me.

We are standing in a large space, surrounded by large steel walls. He seems almost surprised by this. He opens his hands up, and snake-like black spikes slither out, exploring the walls around us.

'You have an immensely powerful mind; whatever it is hiding, it does not want me to find.' His voice echoes inside my head. *'Feel our connection, and let me in. Your subconscious is fighting us.'* With his words, I hold his hand and let myself feel his presence. Calmness fills me as we touch, making my mind feel a sense of comfort. In an instant, a crack appears inside one of the walls, moving from the bottom to the top as it splits a small hole through it.

The stranger lets his darkness seep through, pulling on the barrier more and more, causing the walls to crumble. As he pulls, an image of what appears to be me comes before us.

I close my eyes and count as a small boy runs from me, giggling happily. He crouches behind a small tree. We appear to be in a backyard, just outside of a forest.

'Hide and seek?' I ask him, watching as I suddenly transform into an animal. A small, winged cheetah cub now stood before us. The young boy looked terrified at the transformation, and the cub cowered down in response.

We watch as my mother appears, cursing and calling her a "demon" as she abandons her on the side of the road—the image flickers as I seem to wake up from sleep. The barrier quickly rebuilds itself once more, briefly sending a sense of pain throughout my mind.

'What happened?' I ask him.

'There's something that your mind is hiding from us,' He takes a deep breath before sending more darkness toward the walls. *'This may hurt a bit, but you can trust me.'*

Memories flood my brain fragments and images of me transforming into different creatures and growing my powers as I age. I favor being a dragon, as I do most of the fighting that way.

None of the memories I am shown are whole, cutting off at random times. We learn that my name is "Angel," and I was trained by a black panther named Midnight. We seem to have had a strong bond that only strengthened as I progressed.

One memory, the most fragmented of all, stands out. I was fighting a large army full of the devil's followers. The battle skips and sputters around as I try to approach Lucifer himself. The memory is surrounded in darkness of its own making, as it continuously fights the stranger as he tries to unravel it. I watch in horror as I appear to stab myself with a blade, only for the barrier to become even stronger as we try to pry. Pain shoots throughout my body, causing me to panic. The stranger suddenly takes his grip off me, causing us both to stumble as we leave my mind.

"I don't understand. Everything is so jumbled; what am I blocking from us?" I sigh, running my fingers through my hair, trying to understand.

"Well, Angel, you could see the amount of training you have. Your mind is powerful, and it does not want us to see what caused the anguish inside of you. We made great progress nevertheless."

"Angel," Lana repeats, staring at me with caring eyes. "It is a beautiful name," Her attention turns toward her husband. "Cobra, could we watch over this one? She is clearly in need." *Cobra.* I repeat to myself.

Chapter Two

Lucifer

Lucifer stares at her, curiosity in his eyes. He never understood why she wouldn't wake up; he thought he had healed her enough. The wound in her breast is as healed as possible, apart from the terrible scar now dampening her perfect figure. Even his magic couldn't completely heal her from a strike from the sword; it was a creation of God himself. He never expected her to want to end her own life, and letting her die felt like a waste. Part of him was glad that the cat had stopped her in time.

Angel is quite beautiful; there is no denying it. Her dirty-blonde waves gently rested on her chest, the ends barely hanging over the sides of the bed she was on. The black dress he had his demons put her in fit her body well, complementing the curves of her body. Her now black wings match it perfectly, giving her a frightening, demonic appearance.

Someone might mistake her for dead at first glance. Her breaths are so long and slow that her chest barely moves. Her body is completely still, with not a single twitch to be seen. It is a confusing sight.

How she aged was strange; her body still grew in its coma-like state, feeding only off her power. She had laid there for four years, completely motionless yet alive. *Is she really alive?* He asks himself. He could hear her heartbeat clear as day, pumping magical blood through her veins. He had tried to puncture her mind again, but it was empty. It was as if she had erased herself. *Is he protecting her?* He asks, a shiver running down his spine at the thought. *No, that's impossible.* He assures himself. God would not interfere in such a way; that's not how He works.

Lucifer knew little about her magic, just that it was rather powerful and terrifying. He would have never believed that she would be capable of such destruction had he not seen him himself. In all her agony, she wiped out his entire army with a heartfelt scream. He couldn't understand how she had done it, but it had ruined years and years of his progress. The image of her green death shooting through his slaves constantly ran through the back of his mind.

It had taken him years to rebuild his army, finding lost souls to trick into joining his cause. It still wasn't as big as it had been. He knew there was a long way to go.

With Angel no longer in the picture, he had set his minions free into the world, doing as they pleased and spreading fear. It was fascinating to watch; the humans first gave him a strong fight, sending all their armies after his dragons and killing one with a few lucky missile shots.

It did not take them long to eradicate the armies, though. Once that happened, most humans hid, leaving those above the ground defenseless and his for the taking.

Still, Lucifer wanted more power. Since Angel's mind felt empty, a part of him longed for her to wake up; her empty mind could make it easy for him to convince her to join his cause. She would destroy his army; no one would want to fight her if she was at his side. *But would she join me?* He ponders to himself. Maybe he should just kill her instead, save himself the risk of her remembering.

No. He reminded himself. *She is far too valuable, even if she doesn't join me. Just the chance…it's all I need.*

"Pardon the intrusion," One of his demons walks into the room, fear in his eyes. He was told never to bother him in this room, for it was the only time Lucifer was alone.

"Before you continue, is it worth losing your life?" Lucifer snaps, his eyes not leaving Angel's body.

"Well, I just wanted to tell you we finally found it." The man whispers, almost inaudibly. Lucifer's head turns toward him, hope filling his eyes.

"Give it to me, now." He commands, eagerness in his voice. They had been searching for it for quite some time. That vile cat was very good at keeping it hidden, changing the location every few months.

The man disappears for a moment, only to return with a sword in his hands, concealed in its sheath. Lucifer snatches it immediately, ordering the man to go.

"The sword of shapeshifters," he says, carefully holding the concealed blade. "Now, no one will stand in our way." He places it on a table next to Angel, being sure not to lay a finger on the blade. If someone not worthy touched the sword, it would disappear completely, patiently awaiting its next holder. He could not allow it to go into another shapeshifter's hands again.

A sudden change in Angel's heartbeat makes him swing himself around. She lets out a soft gasp, making his heart leap. He watches breathlessly as her body momentarily arches, her wings stretching to both sides. Within a second, her body relaxes, returning to its resting state. He rushes to her, reaching for her mind. *Nothing... Where are you?* He asks himself, watching curiously as her body rests as it had before.

Chapter Three

Fractured

"Let's keep trying," I say to Cobra, closing my eyes again. We had been sitting in the grass for hours, meditating with our hands joined as he tried to piece together my fragmented memories. Every time he tried, pain surged throughout my body like stinging needles. I just keep hoping it will be worth it.

"I don't want to hurt you any more than I have to." He says, seeming not to want to go any farther.

"Please, I need to know. It's all so confusing." I plead. Although I could see bits and pieces of myself, nothing was truly whole. I could see who I used to be, but I did not feel like them despite how much I wanted to. "Just one more time." He sighs, sending his darkness throughout my mind once more. I straighten my back and take deep breaths as my head pounds, sending pain throughout my body. I could no longer see the memories Cobra was trying to reach, trying my best to stay connected with him as he dug deeper.

'There's someone here,' He whispers through the pain. *'He is hidden, surrounded by darkness.'*

'Can you reach him?' I ask, trying my best to ignore the fire throughout my body.

'Not without causing us both harm.' Cobra replies, his uneasiness

reaching me.

'I can handle it.' I say confidently, bracing myself for more. He lets out a sigh before sending more of his darkness into me.

* * *

Lana sits patiently on a stump near Angel and Cobra, using her connection to her husband to understand what is happening. It was almost too much to bear.

Cobra reaches farther into the barrier, pulling at the memory of some human. He was just a boy, pure and loving and full of optimism. Angel's connection with him radiated; it filled the memory with strength. He stood before the fragments of her memories, guarding them with a powerful sword. It seemed to have a strong connection to him and Angel, fueling the boy with its power.

As Cobra faces the stranger within Angel's mind, her entire body tenses up. He filled her body with so much darkness she couldn't handle it. *How is the memory so strong?* Lana questions herself. People from Earthly planets should not be this strong. Something else was clearly at work here. It was divine.

Lana covers her mouth as she watches Angel's wings turn pitch black, all the checkered whiteness now gone. Blood starts to drip from her nose, softly dropping into the grass. She swallows hard, her jaw clenching tightly as she fights the pain. Lana straightens herself up, unsure as to stop them or not.

Cobra lets out a wet cough, sending a trickle of blood from his mouth. Lana immediately jumps to her feet, rushing toward them both. She had seen enough of this.

"Cobra, stop. You're making her fade. She's not ready!" She calls out, watching Angel's appearance waver between being transparent and solid. Cobra's eyes shoot open, and he releases Angel's hands, letting out a few coughs.

"You're right; she is far from it. This one has seen terrible things." He whispers, watching Angel shake her head, trying to regain her senses.

* * *

"What did you see?" I ask Cobra, having no recollection of what had happened.

"There are many memories within you that can't be reached, at least not yet," Cobra replies, seeming to be in deep thought.

"Can we at least try?"

"Not without great injury to you, possibly even death. There's someone very dear to you, guarding your memories. But it seems like you have blocked them off for some reason." *Someone dear to me…I wish I could remember.*

"Perhaps that is what's making my memories all jumbled. Is there anything I can do to become strong enough to handle it?" I ask him, desperation in my voice.

"Perhaps. We will have to focus on your strength. We have seen bits and pieces of you fighting. Do you think you could handle some combat? It might help you unlock some memories." He asks me.

"I think so. I mean, after all, I've seen myself do." I reply to him, trying to reach for memories of combat. Cobra draws his sword, eyeing me carefully.

"No, let me." Lana comes between us, giving Cobra a look before turning toward me. In a moment, she transforms into a massive silvery wolf towering above the both of us. Energy radiates off her as she changes, her body fueled by some sort of power. She stretches her legs, looking down at her paws and closing her eyes. In an instant, they turn into dark blue ice. *Woah.* I think to myself, staring at her with open amazement. *How am I supposed to fight that?* Lana lifts her head, her eyes meeting mine. "Mana is the only way I can hit you. It'll help you focus." She says gently, patiently waiting for me.

Oh, it must be my turn. I nod at her, taking a few steps back as I try to dig into my mind. *There must be something in me that'll show how I turn.* Memories of turning into a wolf and running through the forest flood my brain. *Perfect.* I say to myself, concentrating hard on getting my body to change as Lana's did.

In an instant, I transform into a white wolf about half her size. I give her a proud look, feeling stronger in this new form of mine. Lana narrows her eyes slightly and lowers herself, an almost playful smile forming on her lips. Cobra takes a few steps back, observing us as we leap toward each other.

As we collide, my mind floods with images of battles between a large black panther, who I assume to be Midnight, and me. I reach for them, trusting my body to remember how it used to fight. In an instant, I reach a memory of the two of us in the middle of a spar.

'You must be faster than that, Angel. Strength is not everything.' Midnight warns, easily avoiding my next strike. 'I think I am starting to understand how you managed to fight shapeshifters.' I reply in a weak tone, feeling out of breath. Midnight's lips curl into a mischievous smile, and she gestures for me to attack again.

I lunge at her, going for the side. She immediately jumps out of the way, turning around to face me. A moment too late, as I use my wings to propel myself into her, making us tumble through the grass.

I manage to pin her down once we stop, her green eyes staring back at me with a glimmer of pride.

'The protégée has finally—' Midnight maneuvers herself faster than expected, rolling us so she's now the one doing the pinning.

'Never let your guard down, Angel. Haven't I told you before?' She replies with a stern voice with a hint of annoyance.

My ears ring slightly as Lana comes back into view, watching me with concern. "What is it?" She questions.

"I remember her…Midnight." I say gently, letting the vague memory fill my mind. "I saw her fighting me. We were training. We shared a strong bond. I think…I think she tried to save me when I…" I trail off, losing my thoughts once more. *What is wrong with me?* I question, annoyance building inside. I give my head a shake and immediately leap toward Lana, hoping our battle will make my mind connect itself some more.

After about thirty more minutes of back-and-forth dueling, Lana finishes me off by pinning me into the dirt and giving me a fake growl. *Just like Midnight. Will I ever learn?* I could tell she was going easy on me the entire time; she was much stronger in her wolf form.

"Did this help?" She asks me, letting me get back on my feet.

"I think so. I have a better picture now, thank you. That was kind of fun." I say to her, gently brushing against her fur with a soft shove.

"It was, wasn't it? But no more games," She turns to Cobra,

"Should we take her to the group now? We've already wasted so much time. Surely the Metallic Empire knows of her presence now."

Metallic Empire? I ask myself, curious as to what that all meant. Cobra nods and jumps onto Lana's back effortlessly despite her massive height.

Without a word, they take off into a run. "Thanks for the warning." I groan, doing my best to keep up with them. This seems to be an almost impossible task, as Lana seems to get faster with each stride. After a few minutes, Lana is nearly out of view, though I am running as fast as I possibly can. Memories of me being a dragon flood my mind. *Surely I should know how to fly?* I say to myself, quickly coming to a stop. I concentrate on the image of a dragon, thinking of its massive size and powerful wings.

Within a moment, my body transforms into a scaley beast. My heart sinks as I notice the size of the wings attached to my back. They are much bigger than in my human form. *I fought like this.* I assure myself, feeling the immense power of being a dragon. I focus my eyes on where Lana is, noticing she is long gone. *I can admire my size later.* I say to myself, remembering that I am lost without them.

With one simultaneous kick of the ground and stroke of my wings, I am in the air. I focus most of my energy on my wings, trying to move as fast as possible in Lana's direction. I move almost effortlessly through the air, trusting my muscle memory to do the work.

The landscape before me catches my attention, nearly taking my breath away as I soar. Large fields of grass were before me, leading up to distant mountains. Everything seems so small from up here. *I know why I use my wings so much now.* I say to myself, enjoying the sensation of the wind under my wings. *Focus.*

As I scan around me, I notice Lana and Cobra standing amongst a small group of people in the distance; it is much easier to see up here. I slow my momentum down some, slowly descending toward them. Within a few moments, I land softly next to them, trying to ignore all of their piercing eyes. Still in her wolf form, Lana walks up to me again, not seeming slightly surprised at my new appearance.

"Don't be frightened; they are friendly…for the most part." She tries to ease the tension. "That one there actually has the same name as you, Angel. She is an excellent sniper. The big guy is Zack. He is our strongest fighter. The woman with the helmet is Hera, and the one with the long dark hair is Diamond, Cobra's sister. Lastly, the two over there are Ace and Dana." She gives me a quick introduction to everyone.

I focus my attention on them, opening my mind toward them. They feel strong, ready for anything that comes their way. *Let's see what I can find out.* I think to myself, my eyes shifting toward the sniper. She is sitting atop a rock, looking out into the distance. I tense up momentarily as my mind connects to hers, feeling her heart beat in rhythm with every breath she takes. *I can hear her thoughts; I can feel her!* I think excitedly, my attention turning toward the biggest guy in their group.

He is standing guard, his weapon on the ground. His mind is going over plans on how to kill a metallic soldier, whatever that is. *'Dense. Heavy, slow attacks. Weak in the joints.'* He lists to himself. I focus on his heart, beating like he is constantly adrenaline-filled.

I shift my eyes toward the girl with the helmet, standing close to Cobra's side. She stands idly by, her weapon drawn. *She must be his guard.* I think to myself as I reach for her mind. *That's strange.* I think, noticing the emptiness of her mind.

My attention goes to the girl with long hair, Cobra's sister. She is eyeing the ground, collecting rocks. *'Just because a rock is broken doesn't mean it doesn't deserve to be collected.'* She says to herself as she plucks one from the ground. Her heart beats normally, filling her with warmth. I try not to smile as I watch her, feeling almost protective. *This is incredible. Did I do this often?* I ask myself, eager to find out more.

The couple quietly talking caught my attention. I look toward the man, focusing on his mind. *'We should be more careful who we let in the group.'* His words make my eyes shift down, trying not to draw his attention. His heart beats calmly beside his woman. She seems incredibly different than him, full of energy and light.

'We will be safe. We are together and will get through this, especially my bebes.' She encourages herself, her body full of excitement and nerves.

"They aren't far." Cobra says, breaking my concentration. He motions for his group to get ready. They immediately spread out, each preparing themselves for whatever is coming.

A shiver runs down my spine as five perfectly oval portals appear. They are completely gray and unwavering. Whatever made them is clearly advanced; it is coming right for us. Pairs of soldiers walk out from each portal, moving slowly and heavily with every step. They are large and thick, covered in black armor that appears to be made of chitin—metallic *soldiers.* I conclude.

As they run at us with great haste, more memories flood my brain of the battle I was in, full of many different dragons. I immediately take to the skies, still in my dragon form. *There are too many.* I think to myself.

I focus my attention on Cobra and his group, watching them fight. They were a team, working together and following his lead. They form a circle, with Cobra in the middle. They are holding their ground well, slashing away at the soldiers individually. But they are outnumbered.

My eyes widen at Cobra's darkness seeping out of him, connecting to his group. They all appear stronger with his touch, their movements becoming quicker and heavier. *Extraordinary.* I think to myself.

Cobra remains out of the fight as his friends become empowered by his darkness. *I'm curious what his plan of attack is.* I look into his mind, full of pain and anguish, yet he seems so calm.

Noticing how strong and durable the enemies are, it becomes clear that his empowerment won't last very long. Determined to help, I reach deep within my chest for power. I instantly find it, a surging fire begging to come out. I open my jaws wide and let out a jew of purple flames. The ground before me becomes covered in dense smoke, giving them the necessary cover. I circle, trying to get a glimpse of someone. *Why is this smoke so thick?* I question not being able to see a thing. Clashing metal and sniper shots fill my ears as they battle beneath me.

I gasp as I feel Cobra's darkness give out; they don't have much time now. Panicked, I move lower to get a better look. By the time I can make them out, it is too late. The soldiers overcome the group with swords plunged into their bodies. All of them except Ace and Hera fall to the ground, appearing dead.

I stay frozen as I watch the soldiers close in on Hera. *How could someone so powerful just...die?* I question myself. Cobra's darkness felt so vital to me; it was terrifying.

Before I can move to help Hera, every downed person in the group suddenly opens their eyes. Each one has a unique color in their eyes, Lana's being pure white, *just like when I first came here.* I remember thinking about how different she looked before pulling me through.

They all slowly rise back up, the energy off them shaking me to the core. They are not what they were before; their bodies feel as though they're pulsing with evil energy. I would have evaded them without a second thought if we weren't fighting on the same side. *These are still the same people; you can feel them.* I remind myself, snapping out of my fear and preparing to join back in the fight.

I swoop down toward them, determined to help in any way I can. I dive at a soldier, extending my claws as I latch onto his shoulders. He struggles within my grasp, swinging violently as I carry him up. Once I am high enough, I fling him to the side as I release my hold. He tumbles toward the ground, away from the fight.

I immediately fly back toward their circle, trying to lessen the number of soldiers around them.

This tactic doesn't help for long, as the group begins to separate more and more as they fight endlessly with the flow of enemies. Worry fills me as I watch, desperately picking away at the soldiers. My eyes focus on Lana, whose eyes are still that pure white color I saw before. She is surrounded by three soldiers, doing her best to keep them at bay. *It's still her.* I remind myself once more.

A wave of encouragement starts to consume me. I let out a piercing roar before diving at one of the soldiers behind her. He tries to pierce me with his sword, but it goes straight through; I am not truly here after all. He pushes himself out from underneath me, motioning toward one of the other soldiers, who immediately runs off. Ignoring this, I sink my teeth into him, struggling momentarily to pierce his armor's protective shell. I give his body a few hard shakes before casting it aside. Lana gives me a proud smile before colliding with another soldier.

I turn to help her, stopping dead in my tracks as the sound of ripping fills my ears. My body freezes up as a familiar shiver runs down my spine. It was as though the sky above me was splitting open.

Before I can react, a large soldier lands hard on my back. A rod plunges through me, causing me to fall to my knees in my human form. A sense of dizziness overcomes me as a portal appears, just a tiny sliver of one. As panic sets in, Cobra touches my side with his darkness, instantly coming into my mind.

'Trust me.' He whispers. *'I can handle this; just let me in.'*

'I trust you.' I reply, closing my eyes and opening up to him as best I can.

Cobra immediately unleashes his darkness inside me, taking control of my body. Calmness fills me as he lets his darkness flow through me. It shatters the barriers within my mind almost immediately, sending a wave of pain throughout my being.

I try to scream as my memories become woven together once more. Images of Justin's bleeding body flash through my mind. A distorted voice calling in my head, 'and you're dead!' Cobra's calming hold on me increases significantly, making me numb as I watch my worst fears play throughout my mind.

'Just a little longer.' He tells me, sending his darkness into the rod still piercing me. As it becomes filled with darkness, it starts to corrupt. It sends out a small but powerful blast, knocking the soldier on my back off.

'You're going to need this. Let it strengthen you.' Cobra says fiercely as he leaves my mind, taking almost all of his darkness. As the calmness leaves, my mind fills with devastation, and my body shakes violently. *I killed him...I killed him...* I repeat myself, barely feeling Cobra throw me through the portal just before it closes.

Chapter Four

Darkness

My ears ring, and my head pounds as I open my eyes. I immediately reached where the rod had been, finding nothing but a slight itching feeling. *That was some dream.* I sigh in relief, trying to ignore the cold feeling looming over me. *It was a dream, right?* I questioned myself, the thought like poison in my head. I close my eyes, flushing the idea out. *Impossible. There isn't more than one dimension.*

I slowly sit myself up, my muscles aching with every movement. I look at my surroundings, trying to understand where I could be. I am seated on a hard, cool mat in the corner of a large dark room with little light. It is almost empty here, except for a single table and a long mirror. I bring my hands into my lap, stopping to notice my attire. I am in a long, black dress covered in cracks with orangish-red tints, making it look like hot coals—the thought of someone else clothing me makes my stomach turn.

I stretch my arms into the air as I let my wings extend, a soft sigh escaping me. I glance at them, noticing their new appearance. They are almost entirely white, but every feather has a pure black tip. *That seems fitting enough.* I think to myself, trying to keep the image of Justin out of my head. I have more important things to worry about right now. I pull myself onto my feet and nearly fall, the quick movement sending a dizzy spell over me.

"Jeez, how long has it been?" I ask myself as I regain my balance. My attention goes to the mirror on the other side of the room. *There's only one way to tell.* I think to myself, slowly moving my stiff joints toward it. My heart sinks as I approach. It is clear that time has passed; my chest is more swollen and perked up, and my figure is tall and curvier. *I look like Emily.* I think to myself, the image of my sister lingering in my mind. *I hope she is okay.*

My eyes still have their green shimmer, but a dullness fills them. It seems fitting enough, given how weak I feel. As I stare, a small flash of black through my eyes makes me shake my head and close my eyes for a moment. I move slightly closer to the mirror and stare intently, seeing only green. I let out a sigh of relief before taking a glance at my hair. It is incredibly long, flowing down to just above my wide hips. *Just a dream. But so was the one of you killing Justin.* I challenge myself, hating how much I denied those nightmares. *He could still be alive if you had listened.*

A loud 'clunk' from outside the room sends me a ping of anxiety, making me remember I have no idea where I am. I can contemplate the meaning of my dreams later. I scan the room around me quickly, trying to see if there is anything I can use to help me, just in case. With my eyes adjusted to the room's darkness, I bring my attention to the table.

I freeze at the sight of a familiar sheath, a shiny green emerald catching my eye. "It can't be," I whisper, going over to it. I slowly pull it from the table. Tears slide down my cheeks as I examine it for a moment, hearing it softly hum to me. *Whose house am I in? Why would they keep it with me?* I ask myself, gently pulling it from its sheath. Hope fills me as I think of Midnight; maybe she is the one that put me in here.

The sword shimmers brilliantly in the dark, emitting a soft green glow. I trace the emerald with my finger, closing my eyes as an image of Justin pops into my mind.

He is holding the sword before me in Midnight's dark cave.

"This sword is an angel killer," he quietly says, promptly setting it beside himself.

"Yes, it could end any chance of defending the world from evil shifters in the wrong hands. But since the sword didn't deny you, I know you are the right holder for it. Now you just have to learn how to use the thing." She says, moving toward the exit of the cave.

"I can't keep this. It could kill you." He tries to put it back, but I grab the handle, sending a shiver down my spine. I had never felt something so frightening before.

"You have to. Let's just see how sharp this thing is," I hand it to him, showing the palm of my hand. He hesitates but gently lays the tip of the sword down on me, instantly showing blood. I rip my hand back as quickly as I can. *"Well, that will be the only time we ever try that out,"* I say, wrapping my hand up with a piece of my shirt and taking a few deep breaths.

"That's going to leave a scar," Midnight says, watching me as I inspect my hand.

I take a deep breath and open my eyes, pushing the memory away. My eyes linger on my palm, the small white scar still there.

"I'm so sorry," I whisper, sliding it back into its sheath. I strap it to my waist, tying the belt tightly so it won't slip. I take a deep breath before making my way toward the door.

I press my ear against it, trying to listen if anyone is around me. Hearing nothing, I attempt to turn the knob. To my surprise, the door opens. *Am I not locked in here? Although, it wouldn't stop me.* I say to myself as I crack it open slightly, peering into a long narrow hallway. Seeing no one, I slip through the door and creep down the hall, moving as fast and light as possible. I have no idea who my captor is, and I do not want to risk being caught.

As I reach the edge of the hall, voices fill my ears, and the hair on my arms stands on end. *Minions.* I think to myself, letting the familiar warning fill my body. *Looks like it wasn't Midnight.*

"When will he be back?" A man's voice asks.

"Soon enough. Let's hurry up and check on the girl before heading out. You know how he is rather fond of her." The other man replies. I quickly turn around and slip through another door. *Fond of her?* I question why someone would be sending guards to check on me.

"What's the point? She only sleeps." Annoyance fills his voice as he follows his colleague.

I stand quietly, listening to their footsteps as they walk by. As soon as they're past, I run back out, increasing my speed as it is only a matter of seconds before they realize I am gone.

I make my way down the hallway, running as fast as my legs can carry me, determined to find an exit. A door at the very end of it is cracked open slightly, calling for me to go through. After a few moments, I reach it and push it open, revealing a large room with a few men standing in it. Their eyes widen as if they had seen a ghost.

No one moves a muscle as a painfully familiar voice screams, "Where is she?!?" His words echo throughout the halls, full of rage. Ignoring the bone-chilling coldness I now feel, I take a deep breath and slowly walk through the room toward the men who seem unsure about what to do.

I feel the sword's hilt and draw it from the sheath, holding the blade close to my body as I walk, trying to give them all threatening glances. I spread my wings into the air to make myself appear bigger. There was no way I was going to let Lucifer keep me here.

"Don't just stand there. Someone grab her!" An older man shouts, prompting a younger guy to run in my direction. I stop for a moment and ready the sword, trying to ignore the weakness I feel. *This sword can cut through anything.* I remind myself, praying it does its job. All of my sword fighting with Justin has to count for something. As he reaches me, I hop to the side and slash him with it, easily cutting through his flesh. *Smooth as butter.* I say to myself, shocked as to how powerful it really is. The sword lets out a soft hum as if pleased with itself. Ignoring the slight dizziness, I now feel, I glare at the other men.

"Anyone else fancy a try?" I mock them, holding the now bloodied blade in front of me. The remaining three men take a few steps back. "That's what I thought," I say, quickly approaching the rather large exit, keeping the sword ready. A sense of strength comes through, making every step I take easier and easier. A shiver runs down my spine as I reach the warehouse door, prompting me to turn around.

"Angel! Don't you dare. We can talk about this." Lucifer commands, eyeing me carefully from across the room with devilish eyes.

"No, don't you dare. You were foolish enough to keep the sword with me. Now watch as we both leave your grasp." I fiercely reply, smiling at him as I spin myself around. I kick hard on the garage door, making it fly off its frame and into the air. Whatever is strengthening me doesn't seem to want to stop just yet. A hot burst of air comes in, dry heat and blinding light now before me. I shift into my cheetah form, the sword disappearing with my clothes as I change.

Feeling the energy quickly fill and rejuvenate my being, I take off into a sprint. Lucifer shouts commands at the men behind me, panic filling his voice. I leap into the sky and spread my wings, instantly gaining altitude. The feeling of my wings in the air sends a sliver of hope throughout me. I dare not look back as I climb into the sky, feeling the presence of Lucifer's minions close behind me.

One of them breathes hot flames in my direction, prompting me to dive out of their way. He dives after me, his presence dangerously close. Just before I reach the ground, I spread my wings and go into a painful glide as my paw skims the sand below. The dragon behind me wasn't so lucky; he collided with the earth, sending bits of sand everywhere.

I look back for a moment, watching as he shakes the sand off and scowls at me. Another minion is close behind, flying just over his downed friend.

I tilt myself up and begin to climb. I don't stop until the air thins, pumping my wings with every bit of strength I have left. As I level out, I let my eyes wander and take in the vast landscape. I am somewhere in the desert, surrounded by nothing but sand and rock.

I feel for the presence of the minions, finding nothing. My speed had saved me this time.

"Lucifer had me… and didn't kill me," I say to myself, feeling safe enough to relax as I glide through the air. I must conserve as much energy as I possibly can. I doubted his new minions could fly as fast as me, especially at this altitude. Unsure of where I am headed, I let my wings guide me as I fly, catching various air currents to carry me through the sky.

Chapter Five

Open Waters

By the time the sun sets, I find myself on a shoreline with nothing but an open ocean in front of me. Knowing there was no way I could fly across the water right now, I let myself fall hard into the sand.

I shift back into my human form, immediately reaching for the sword. Thankfully, it is still safely attached to my waist. *That's good to know.* I think, spreading myself out on the sand as I relax. It doesn't take long for my exhausted body to succumb to sleep, soothed by the sounds of the crashing waves.

The dryness of my throat wakes me; flying through an endless desert has made me somewhat dehydrated…and I have no idea how long I was asleep. I focus on the salty water, noticing how welcoming it seems. I have never seen the ocean before, but I have heard that saltwater will only make you thirstier if you try to drink it. *I am not a human.* I remind myself, letting my thirst lead me to the water's edge.

A wave comes up and gently kisses my feet with a warm touch before seeping back into the deep as it leaves a trail of foam. I take a few more steps to where the water is just below my knees and crouch down. If I were hydrated at all, surely my mouth would be watering.

Compelled by my thirst, I cup my hands and bring a handful of water to my mouth, taking a small sip. I immediately spit it out in disgust. I gaze toward the sky, staring gloomily at the millions of stars lighting it. "Why am I still alive?" I whisper, taking a deep breath as I try to ignore the weakness I feel.

Distant splashes catch my attention, causing me to gaze toward the dark water. A few sea creatures jump out of it repeatedly as if playing in the moonlight. They don't seem to have a care in the world. *It would be nice to be like them.* I think to myself as a new idea comes to mind.

"I wonder," I say, standing up and making my way deeper into the salty water. It feels surprisingly warm on my skin, welcoming me with an open embrace. I follow my thirsty urge, transforming myself into a bottlenose dolphin.

The sensation is much different than any transformation I have done before, as my legs and arms shrink considerably, turning into flippers. Trying to get used to this new body, I move in a few small circles. *This is easy enough.* I think, noticing how easily I am propelled around.

I cautiously open my jaws and take another drink, expecting the same salty taste. Instead, it has a smooth and soothing taste, relieving my body. *Finally,* I think to myself, enjoying the feel of the refreshing water.

Once I quench my thirst, I move deeper into the ocean, gliding effortlessly through the water. The world around me is mesmerizing; many colorful fish swim around me, darting every which way whenever I get too close. I am a predator, after all.

A large boat zooming above causes most of the creatures around me to take off in a hurry, the loud engine ringing through our ears. Once it safely passes, I make my way to the surface to get some air, feeling relieved to see the sun starting to rise.

The sound of a dolphin pod coming near draws my attention. They slowly start to make their way toward me, curiosity filling them as they do so. They call out happily, singing and jumping through the water. I try to stay still as a young dolphin swims up, gently brushing against my side.

"Go back to your momma," I say in a distorted voice. In an instant, the baby does exactly that. *That was weird.* I say to myself, watching curiously as the dolphins around me stay still, their eyes on me.

I quickly swim down before turning back up toward the surface, moving as fast as possible. Once I breach it, I shift into my human form, flying up into the sky as the water falls from my body. I hover momentarily before realizing the sheath had slipped off my waist. Panicked, I scan the water, only to notice one of the dolphins holding the sword up on the surface, balancing it with its nose. It lets out a happy squeal as I gently grab it.

"Thank you," I whisper, shock filling me as the pod disappears into the water. *How fascinating.* I think, tying the now wet sheath around my waist again. I fly up into the sky, traveling away from Lucifer and his minions.

I let my mind go blank as I fly, relying on my body to guide me across the vast water. The only sounds within my ears are the soft waves below and the gentle flaps of my wings. A few air currents here and there carry me some, allowing me to glide for most of the time.

By the time the sun sets and begins to rise once more, I notice land on the horizon. Excited, I push my wings to their limit and begin to fly as fast as I can toward it. My wings give out as I go in for the landing, causing me to tumble onto the beach. I lay there momentarily and let my body relax, only to feel weak. I have yet to eat, and my stomach is determined to let me know. The seawater could only do so much.

I slowly stand up after an hour or so, letting my eyes wander the area around me. It's a relatively nice beach, large and warm as the sun rises higher in the sky. Quite a few buildings litter the area behind it. I am clearly in a city of some sort. *Where is everyone?* I wonder, unsure as to why no one would be out on such a beautiful day.

I dust the sand off my dress and shake my wings before heading toward the city. It is incredibly quiet; only a couple of cars here and there drive on the roads, and none of them seem to be obeying traffic laws. The streets are littered with trash, and cars sit on the sides of the roads, some with smashed windows and doors left open. A street sign catches my attention, reading 'Miami.' *Florida.*

I make my way toward a gas station; its windows boarded up, the door reinforced with metal chains. Curiosity and my stomach guiding me, I kick one of the windows in. The board goes flying into the building, causing a woman to let out a loud shriek from within.

"It's okay! I'm sorry, I just need some food." I call to her, slowly climbing through the window. The store is relatively preserved, with shelves full of snacks and things. "I promise I won't hurt you... I can help you fix the window." I say to her as I look around. I notice a few cups of noodles on the shelf and happily grab them along with a bottle of water. "Do you have a microwave?" I call her, filling the noodles with bottled water.

"It's in the back of the store," She replies, slowly revealing herself from behind the counter. Her eyes widen at the sight of me. "Wha–"

"I am Angel; please don't be alarmed. It's been a long journey." I sigh, slowly walking toward her with my hands raised.

"You're real! But you look so different than on the news…I thought your wings were pure white? And that you were a kid?" Her voice quickens as she leads me toward the back of the store.

"They were. This mixed coloration I have now resulted from something of my own doing. It's a constant reminder." I say to her, placing the noodles inside of the microwave.

"Why were you gone for so long? Things have changed." Her voice grows cold.

"I was asleep, in a coma, I believe. I am unsure how long it was, but it was clearly too long. Can you tell me what happened here?" I ask her. She nods her head slowly and offers me a seat on her couch.

She tells me that after the battle with Lucifer, he hid for about three years, only to return to Earth with a growing army of dragons. They fly around the world, causing mayhem and destruction wherever they go. The United States government unleashed the Department of Defense, which had experience with shapeshifters before, but it only made Lucifer angrier.

His army has continually attacked humans, appearing at large gatherings and creating havoc. It has led many people to go into hiding. Most appear to be in bomb shelters, trying to wait it out. Some, such as herself, stay with their businesses/ family homes hoping to remain quiet and undetected. Her story makes the blackness in my chest grow; my mind instantly blames myself.

"If I had succeeded…and not fallen into his trap…" I sigh, staring coldly at the ground. "So many people would still be alive." My mind shifts to Justin momentarily, tears swelling as I push the image away.

"I don't think anyone blames you; we hardly knew anything about you. Besides, you were just a kid! Heck," She eyes me up and down. "You still look pretty young to me." I give her a weak smile.

"Has this happened everywhere?" I ask her. She gives me a slow nod. My mind goes blank for a moment before the thought of Maggie enters it. *Maggie!* I repeat, immediately jumping to my feet. The woman gives me a startled look. "I just remembered someone. I must go now, thank you." I say sternly, making my way back toward the window.

"You're welcome, please… be careful. We need you." She sighs. I give her a slight nod before jumping through, immediately taking to the skies. Feeling rejuvenated from finally eating, I quickly climb into the clouds in seconds. Hiding up here would be the safest spot for me, for I had a feeling that Lucifer would be searching.

I let my body guide me as I fly as fast as I can through the clouds, an ounce of hope within my chest that Maggie may still be alive. I just had to get to her.

After about three hours, I find myself slowly starting to descend. As I leave the clouds, I notice a familiar forest below me. *Dark Pines Forest, where I grew up…* My mind trails off as I softly land in a large clearing. It is hushed here as if all the wildlife had disappeared. The ground before me was a mess, full of tree branches and torn grass. Everything here is dead.

A small opening in the ground catches my attention—a *cave.* My heart sinks as I realize where I ended up. Midnight's cave is completely quiet, the opening covered in the destruction of this once beautiful meadow. *Our meadow.* I repeat, no longer able to fight the memories clawing at my head. *I killed him here. I let everyone down in this very spot…* The barriers I have been trying so hard to keep suddenly crumble, making me fall to my knees. I dig my fingers into the ground before me, letting my wings go limp as I let it out.

My body shivers as I clutch the dirt, sobbing uncontrollably. Many thoughts fill my head, pointing to the words my mother once called me: 'demon.' I lift my head for a moment to catch my breath, noticing the pure blackness of my wings. *Why do they change so much?* I ask myself, inspecting them. They are as black as night, not a sliver of white within them. *Now these are wings worthy of a demon.*

Chapter Six

Stories

"Angel," A voice pulls me from my slumber. I open my eyes, realizing I am still in the same spot, lying in the dirt. I take a deep breath and stare intently at the ground as I position my hands for a quick jump into the air.

"You're here!" The voice calls, placing a warm hand on my shoulder. I jump up at their touch, swinging around and hitting them hard with my wings as I do so. I face them, narrowing my eyes as they stand back up. My wings go limp as our eyes meet.

"Orion?" I ask him, staring intently at his figure. He is nearly unrecognizable. He is older looking and taller, his arms bulging with new muscles. The shy look on his face was completely gone, replaced by confidence and something else.

"Angel… we thought you were dead." He says, his voice softening.

"I wish I were," I reply coldly, my eyes returning to the ground. His arms embrace me tightly within an instant, causing tears to fall from my eyes unwilfully. He holds me for a few minutes, staying completely silent as I drench his shoulder. "Thank you," I whisper once the tears stop.

"Now," he says, pulling away from the embrace. "We must get out of here. This is the first place anyone would look for you. Besides, the amount of energy you're giving off is insane."

"I'm giving off energy?" I ask him.

"Oh, yes. To be honest, I thought you were Lucifer at first…until I saw you lying there. It's like you carry the same darkness on you." My heart sinks. *Am I giving off dark energy?* "It will be hard for you to hide."

"I can't hide Orion. Have you seen what he has done? I must stop him… It's all my fault." I argue.

"Angel, you listen to me," He starts, his hazel eyes staring into mine. "I was there. That…that thing that you became, it wasn't you. Your eyes weren't this beautiful green. They were pure black; your goodness was drained away. Now, please, let's go. This forest is crawling with minions." I look at him for a moment, trying my best to imagine it. *Pure black eyes…Maybe that shimmer I saw was real.*

"I need to hear more," I reply.

"I will tell you all you want to know if you come with me." He commands, turning himself into a wolf. I reluctantly shift into my silvery wolf form beside him.

"Where else would I go?" I reply. Orion smiles before taking off into a run. I follow closely behind him, letting myself feel a slight sense of joy as we run through the trees. The memory of the first time I ran with him comes to mind. *He was so different back then.* I think to myself, remembering how skittish he was.

We eventually reach yet another familiar place: his farm. Compared to how Florida was, this place seemed to be untouched. A calm aroma filled the air, sending a sense of comfort throughout me as we approached the house. We both shift into our human forms simultaneously as we reach the steps. As I walk, I reattach the sword to my hips, determined never to let it leave my sight. Orion momentarily pauses before he opens the door, giving me a cold stare.

"Before we go in, there's something you should know… My grandmother has passed away. It was about three years ago, peacefully in her sleep." He says gently.

"I'm sorry," I reply, slowly following him inside.

"Don't be; I would rather have her gone that way than deal with the world we are a part of now." He sighs, locking the door behind us. I sit on the couch, giving him an impatient look as I wait for his explanation of the story. He ignores this and makes his way to the kitchen.

"Hey!" I shout to him, promptly making my way over there.

"You should eat first. Besides, I will want to hear yours as well… all of it."

Once we are done eating breakfast, we finally make our way back to the living room. I bring a cup of coffee, realizing Maggie is not here to tell me no. 'Coffee is not for children, even magic ones.' she would say, oh how I longed to hear her voice again.

"So, tell me about how it looked…when I wasn't myself anymore." I tell him, pushing the thought of Maggie out of my mind.

"Well, I'll start from just before, right after you and Justin were separated. The way Lucifer was just standing there, I could tell something was wrong. That moment that you landed in front of him, the dragons we were fighting flew off and landed in that circle around you. While distracted, one picked me up from the ground and carried me into the sky. He held me just right; I could hardly move."

"That must have been awful." I chip in, trying to imagine how helpless he must have felt. We were foolish to let an untrained shapeshifter join us in the fight.

"Not as bad as watching what came next. Once you and Lucifer talked for a moment, all of the dragons around you opened their jaws, and that terrible black smoke covered the whole area around you. You disappeared within it; all we could hear were your screams. I had to look away, only to see Justin slicing the dragon holding him wide open… He was so afraid for you. He called your name; he was trying to calm you." Tears form in my eyes as I try and picture it. *He spent his last moments in fear.* I tell myself.

"He cried out: 'I can't feel her anymore!'. It was heartbreaking. Right after, your screaming stopped. Everything went quiet, and the smoke cleared. You were on your knees, and your wings were pure black…" He trails off momentarily, his eyes locking on the wings on my back. *Like they are now,* I finish his sentence, trying to stay calm to hear the rest.

"Lucifer told you to get into your cheetah form, and you did. Your fur was all matted and almost blurry, wild looking. You were panting extremely hard, and small amounts of smoke came from your mouth. I caught a glimpse of your eyes; they were black and smokey…It was like all that dark smoke absorbed into you."

"It was the most painful thing I have ever experienced," I add, remembering how strong Lucifer's hold on me had been.

"Justin killed probably ten dragons trying to reach you before they all flew up into the sky, giving him a clear path to you. Midnight told him no, but he instantly ran at you, not seeming to care how…demonic you looked. Then, Lucifer said, 'kill.' Your focus went to Justin, who took a few steps backward, shaking his head. Midnight told him to defend himself, but he just kept backing up. Eventually, he dropped the sword and fell to his knees. That armor on him shimmered for a moment before fading away. When the sword fell, your ear twitched, and Justin's face lit up. He didn't care that he just lost the sword's power."

"I don't know what to say. Why would he drop the sword? When I came to, I couldn't believe it was lying there." I reply, trying to grasp what this all means.

"He let you kill him, Angel. He couldn't bring himself to hurt you. He knew you weren't yourself." His words make me sink into the couch. *Why would you let me do such a thing?* I think to myself. *Why.* Tears flow from my cheeks.

"He always believed in me more than I ever did," I say, catching my breath. "What happened after Lucifer carried me away?" I ask him, trying to get the entire story.

"Well, not much, to be honest. Midnight made me leave. She did not want me to be there any longer. She said she couldn't lose another one. She wanted me to be safe, so we parted ways. We haven't seen each other much since then; she comes and goes." He replies.

"I wonder where she is… I want to see his burial so that I can say goodbye…"

"I wish I knew where she was. I have only heard bits and pieces; she was trying rather hard to hide that sword. Seems like she didn't do an excellent job, though." He sighs, gesturing to my waist. *No, she did not.* I agree, wondering how they managed to get it from her in the first place.

"It was in the room I woke up in. I am not sure why they were dumb enough to keep it in there."

"The room you woke up in?" He repeats, hinting that it is my turn to tell a story. I sighed before explaining everything I could remember, from my strange dream with Lana and Cobra to waking up, escaping, and finding my way back here.

Chapter Seven

Home

After a long conversation, Orion leads me to his grandmother's old room. It is relatively large with a rustic theme. Paintings of horses are scattered around the wooden walls, along with a few of the outdoors. The bed frame is made of treated wood, with a large headboard with carved horses in it.

"She really liked horses, huh?" I ask him.

"You could say that," He says gently, watching as I sit on the soft bed. "Feel free to go through the closet, get into something more comfortable." He makes his way to leave.

"Thank you, truly," I reply as he shuts the door behind him. I let myself lay backward, enjoying the comfort the bed has to offer. Only then did I remember I spent the night sleeping on the ground. "Shoot!" I exclaim, jumping up from the bed. I quickly brushed the dust and dirt off from where I was. Luckily my dress hadn't been as dirty as I thought.

I make my way over to the closest door adjacent to the bathroom. It slides open smoothly, revealing a large walk-in closet. A few shelves on the right side catch my attention; it is filled with neatly folded sleeping gowns that appear untouched.

I eagerly slip the ash-like dress off my body, sighing in relief to be out of it. I reach for one of the gowns, eagerly grabbing ahold of one. It feels soft and cool in my hands. A mirror catches my attention, making me gasp as the gown falls from my hands. A revolting scar stretches just above my chest, a perfect line of scarred tissue a few inches long. I trace it with my fingers, remembering how easily the sword had sliced through my flesh. *How am I still alive?* I questioned; I knew I had managed to plunge the sword quite deep before Midnight had reached me. She had told me that a hit from the sword would make me heal like a human. *I can worry about this later.* I decide, noticing how filthy my body is.

With the gown now in hand, I walk toward the master bathroom, eager to wash the past few days off. It takes me nearly an hour to thoroughly cleanse myself, getting all the built-up dust and grime.

When finished, I put my hair into a loose bun atop my head and slipped the gown on, gladly hiding the scar from my sight. I let my body fall onto the bed, eager to lay in an actual bed.

"What's the plan for today?" I ask Orion the following morning. We are both sitting at the kitchen table, enjoying a fresh breakfast. He swallows his bite before smiling.

"I am going to make you loosen up. Do some *real* work."

"Work? Shouldn't we be worrying about the apocalypse outside?" I question, my mind drifting to the woman in the gas station. There is no way I can do anything except worry about Lucifer. Orion lets out a sigh.

"You're not going to worry about anything but yourself right now, okay? How do you expect to take on Lucifer when your mental state is so low?" He challenges, annoyance in his voice.

"It's not about me. The world needs him gone; he's pushed so many into hiding. My health can wait." I snap, putting my silverware down. My appetite had suddenly vanished.

"They have been dealing with this for years. They can handle a little longer. If you want to help them, you must first help yourself, Angel. You are not ready to take that all on right now. Just… give me time. I think I can help you." His words send a fury throughout me.

"I don't care how long they've been dealing with it! Any amount with dragons freely roaming is too long. I must help." I stand to my feet, prompting him to do the same.

"And what will you do? Kill them one by one, no plan, no help, just you against an entire army? You're *weak*. What if Lucifer controls you again? Justin isn't here to snap you out of it." The piercing sound of Justin's name makes me slump back into the chair, letting my face fall into my hands.

"I don't…I don't know…" My voice breaks as tears swell in my eyes. The thought of getting controlled again is terrifying. *I'm already giving off a dark aroma…would that make it easier?* Orion's hand touching my shoulder breaks me from my daze.

"I'm sorry. I didn't mean to trigger anything." He whispers.

"It's fine." I wipe my eyes and stand up again, pushing him to the side. "Let's just do that work you were talking about."

We make our way outside to the barn. The smell of horses fills my nose; I had never been so close to them before. It isn't a good smell; the manure masks most of it. I give Orion an intrigued look as he smiles while deeply breathing. He goes to the big door and slides it open, revealing a long alleyway with stalls on both sides. Happy horses' nickering fills my ears; they seem glad to see him.

He leads me down a hall to the left, leading to a large room with an indoor arena inside. A large pile of hay bales sits neatly in a corner, all on a pallet base. He easily piles two of them onto a wagon and pulls it back where we came from.

"So, all we have to do is give them each three flakes. You see the little doors?" He points toward a small opening in one of the stalls. "There are hay feeders through those. Just throw it right in."

With his words, we start throwing food at all of the horses. None of them seemed bothered by the fact that I had wings, something I did not understand. Once we finished doing this, we changed out all their water buckets. It was a relatively easy task; the two-gallon buckets felt weightless, even full.

"Now what?" I asked him once we were finished with all ten stalls.

"Now they get to go outside. This is the fun part." He smiles, walking toward a large black one. He looks directly into its eyes before continuing: "Bonnie, go straight to your paddock." I tilt my head toward him; *no way would an animal listen like that, right?*

When the horse's stall door opens, she trots toward the exit. I watch in awe as she moves straight toward an open gate and runs through it into the pen. She immediately goes onto the ground and starts rolling in a patch of dirt.

"How did you get her to do that?" I ask in awe. He lets out a small laugh.

"By telling them. Here, why don't you try with Branson." He says, gesturing toward a smaller brown horse with a white stripe down his face.

"I just tell him to go to his pen?" I ask, not trusting that it will work. Orion nods. "Okay…" I approach Branson, who suddenly seems to give me his full attention. *This is not normal.* "Branson," His ears pointed toward me. "Go to your pen and stay there," I say, not believing that he will listen.

"Good, now let him out." Orion commands, his arms crossed loosely across his chest. I slowly undo the latch, and to my astonishment, Branson joins Bonnie.

"Why do they listen like that?" I ask him once we are finished letting them all out.

"Angel, we are shapeshifters. Surely you have noticed. Turning into animals has its perks."

"Animals listen to us?" I ask him, still not understanding.

"Yes. I shift into a mammal, so, in a way, I'm connected to all mammals. They can feel that connection to us. They understand me, and I understand them in a sense. You can shift into pretty much anything, right? So, I would bet that any animal would listen to you." *Any animal?* My mind shifts back to how the dolphin seemed to listen to me. *It actually understood what I said?*

"It seems insane, yet I just saw it with my own eyes," I tell him.

"You still have a lot to learn, don't you?" He replies, gesturing for me to follow him. "We have more to do."

The rest of our work consisted of feeding the goats and chickens. It was relatively easy, just time-consuming. Part of me enjoyed the distraction, it made me feel as though I wasn't completely useless, but I knew what he was doing. The more things I get caught up doing, the less I think about Lucifer. Although I enjoy it, I doubt this tactic will work for long.

Once we finished all the farm chores, Orion insisted we go for a trail ride. He explained that his animals need to be exercised somehow. We grabbed Branson and Bonnie from their pen and had them follow us back into the barn.

"Stay still," I command Branson, gently brushing the rest of the dirt off of him. He sure managed to get quite dirty in that short time he was out. "Now what?" I question Orion, feeling as though my work is finished. He smiles before handing me a bottle labeled 'fly spray.'

"Spray it on him, starting with his legs." He commands, giving me a short demonstration with Bonnie. I follow his lead, spraying Branson in the flies' favorite places. "Good, now, let's go outside," Orion says, leading Bonnie outside the barn without a rope. *No saddle?* I shudder, anxiousness rising within me.

Branson stays completely still as I step onto the mounting block, waiting patiently for me to swing onto him. I follow Orion's lead, grabbing ahold of the mane before swinging my right leg over my horse's back.

"Scoot up a little; you want to be at the base of his withers." *The base of his what?* I repeat, gently sliding forward. Branson feels warm underneath me, filling my mind with calmness as I relax on his back. He doesn't seem to have a care in the world about my wings gently swaying behind me as we begin to walk. Orion leads our way, his horse knowing exactly where we are headed.

"How can we control them without tack?" I call to him as we approach a narrow trailhead.

"Don't you understand yet? Reach into Branson's mind and tell him what to do. Otherwise, you can just sit there and let him follow me. He'll do that too." *Reach into a horse's mind?* I question, looking carefully between his big brown ears that turn every which way. He seems relatively calm, effortlessly carrying me as he ventures into the woods behind his friend.

Hesitantly, I focus my mind on him. In an instant, I am filled with a sense of calmness and trust. His mind is much different than a person's, yet it still has some feelings. It is clear that he is focused on one thing: me. It is as though he is paying attention to everything from my leg on his side to my very breath. His breathing quickens as though he can feel me inside his head.

I close my eyes as I continue to search his mind. His legs feel powerful beneath us, held sturdily by his balanced hooves. I feel his tail swish with every step, gently pressing on his legs. A surge of energy flowed throughout him as though he was ready to go however fast I asked him to.

'Trot.' I say to him, gently grabbing his mane as he quickens his pace, quickly catching up to Orion. I give him a happy smile as we pass before turning my head back toward the trail in front of us. *'Faster.'* I command, prompting Branson to change his stride, going into a canter. My heart leaps as he continues to quicken his pace, feeling the excitement coursing through me. I let go of his mane and raise my arms as we run. *Now this is fun.*

Chapter Eight

Restless

By the time two months had passed, I had gotten relatively used to life on the farm. Orion and I have kept ourselves rather busy with the animals, tending to them and keeping everything in order. Having smaller, less end-of-the-world-type tasks feels good, which is a suitable distraction. Neither of us mentions Lucifer, keeping any real-world talk to the bare minimum. As time goes on, I can feel him piecing my heart back together one fragment at a time.

We spend much of our free time riding his horses through the trails around the property. We try and exercise them all, switching which ones we ride each time. He says that without us making them exercise, they'll become fat and lazy, which is no life for a horse. Spending this time with him makes me feel almost…human. I know if I were one, this is the kind of lifestyle I would want. No crowds. Just me and my animals, and not a soul to tell me what to do. It is devastating to know that this will forever be a fantasy. I am not made to sit on a farm and enjoy life. That is why, as I lay in bed last night, I decided to confront Orion about leaving here. I gave him his time, and now I must start thinking about the real world again. We have little time to waste.

"Whatcha want to do today?" Orion asks me the following morning. I gently place my coffee down and think for a moment. The best way to give the news would be through a trail ride, it is when we are both relaxed, and it does help that it's one of his favorite things to do. It will be better to keep him in a good mood anyways.

"How about we go to the creek? We haven't been there in a while." I suggest. He nods his head in agreement, immediately heading for the door before I get a chance to change my mind. The creek is about a thirty-minute ride away and is beautiful. There is a small river that flows through the woods, leading to a small waterfall. It's a wonderful place to swim, as the water is crystal clear beyond the fall. The water is also nestled in a meadow, surrounded by colorful flowers. It is one of the most peaceful places to be around here.

After washing my cup, I head out the door, catching a glimpse of Branson and Lady, another of Orion's horses, walking into the barn. *I'm going to miss this.* I say to myself, pushing the sorrow out of my mind. This will likely be my last trail ride.

By the time I reach them, Branson is patiently waiting for me at the mounting block.

Once we are safely on, Orion leads us into the forest again. The trail has become quite familiar to me as I have gone down it countless times. It is easily my favorite one. It is narrow, with many twists, turns, and uneven ground, making the ride feel like more of an adventure than anything else.

"You seem to like this," Orion speaks up. I shrug my shoulders before giving Branson a soft pat on the neck.

"It's a good distraction. It makes me almost forget what's going on out there."

"It's good to forget sometimes. I can see a change in you…you're more joyful than before." I let out a soft sigh. *He's going to make this hard.*

"Only because I am not around the destruction." Orion doesn't reply, creating an awkward silence for the rest of the ride to the creek. Once we reach it, I lay myself down near the waterfall and close my eyes. The sounds of the forest had always been calming, especially now. Few things in this life keep me calm, and if I didn't have wings, this would easily be my favorite.

Orion tells the horses to stay in sight before joining me in the grass with a relaxing sigh. I turn myself toward him, noticing how peaceful he seems to be. He has been trying his hardest to distract me these past months, and my heart is thanking him for it. He has given me a sense of…peace, even with the thought of Lucifer lingering in my mind. *Maybe I can still enjoy myself…somehow.* I think momentarily, realizing how relaxing this truly has been for me…how peaceful my small glimpse of everyday life has been. *What am I thinking? This is fantasy. I have to leave today.* I remind myself, knowing there is no way I am staying here any longer. I can't.

"How long has it been?" I ask him, breaking the silence. He stirs beside me, keeping his eyes closed.

"Since what?"

"Since I have been here with you. It has been a couple of months, right?"

"Yes," He pauses for a moment. "It doesn't seem like it's been that long, though." He seems satisfied with his reply. *Okay, here we go.* I encourage myself, sitting up in a rush. Orion opens his eyes and gives me a worried look, sending a ping of guilt throughout me. Still, there is no way I am letting him win me over again.

"Two months, I have let Lucifer's minions run free while I enjoy myself. We have to stop this; I can't wait here anymore." I say to him, the sound of my heart pounding through my head. He slowly sits up, his eyes meeting mine, a stern expression on his face. I take a deep breath as his hands grab mine, holding me in place.

"No, Angel. You gave yourself two months of healing. To better yourself, to rebuild your heart. Don't you remember? The mere mention of the battle brought you to tears." He reminds me, his voice soft and encouraging.

"I know…" I shake the thought of it out of my head. "But I can't sit here and do nothing anymore… I can't." My voice begins to break. Orion gently moves his hands to my face, cupping them as he holds my head up. The sensation makes my face heat some, making me freeze in place.

"Then we won't. Come on; I want to show you something." He whispers, pulling me to my feet. "Branson! Lady! Go home and into your stalls." he commands them. Without another word, both horses take off back toward the barn. I stayed in place, unsure how to react to how close our faces had just been.

Orion shifts into his wolf form, gesturing toward the forest before us, oblivious to my confusion. "Don't be mad; I didn't want to take you here until you were ready. It might be a bit…overwhelming." He starts to excuse himself, a hint of nervousness rising in him. *Over-whelming?* I question, beginning to realize that he wants to go some-where.

"What are you talking about?" I question, tilting my head at him.

"Just…follow me. You'll understand soon enough." He takes off into a run, forcing me to do the same. *Where could he possibly be taking me?* I question as we run deeper into the forest. He leads me through a different area, one I have yet to see somehow. The trees become denser as we go, with less and less light shining through their leaves.

"Where are we going?" I call out to him. He slows his pace down to a walk beside me. "I am not going any further until you tell me."

He lets out a sigh. "You are the most stubborn person I have ever met. We are going to the deepest part of the Dark Pines; the trees are extremely dense. It's a safe place from Lucifer's minions." I tilt my head. I thought I had seen every part of this forest by now.

"It's protected, you'll see." He adds, taking off into a run once more. *Protected?*

After about thirty more minutes, the forest continues to get thicker. Even with my quick reflexes and incredible sight, I become clumsy. Branches scrape against my sides, and my strides get inter-rupted by tripping on the ground below me. Orion also seems to be struggling, as his pace has slowed drastically.

"Okay." He stops in front of a grove of dense trees and bushes you cannot see through. "We are here. Shift into your human form." He commands, turning himself back to a human as well.

"How are we supposed to get through there? I can break the trees, but it will be rather destructive." I suggest, scanning them intensely with my gaze. *How have I never been here before?*

"That won't be necessary." A stranger's voice calls rather sharply. "Orion, what have you done? Why have you brought her here? Her dark energy is as strong as Lucifers!" The woman scolds him. *Where is she?* I ask myself, scanning the forest all around us. *And who is she to scold Orion?*

"Open your eyes, Arkadia! This is Angel, the one that has been prophesied. She is not dead and certainly not evil. She needs some hope, and I know you can give that to her." He says rather angrily, staring directly into the trees ahead of us. I focus my eyes where he appears to be looking; only trees block my path. *What is this?*

"I know who she is. I am not a fool. Her energy is strong. She's not welcome here. I will not have any of our blood lost for her foolish cause." *Foolish cause?* I clench my fists and take a step toward her voice. Orion stretches his arm out in front of me, shaking his head.

"I'm not asking you to fight. Just to let us in, to talk." *Let us in? In where?*

"She will expose us all; the energy is too strong." She says, unbending.

"Expose you all? Who are you?" I ask her, followed by an angry glance from Orion. There is no way I am being silent any longer. I don't care who it is.

"Just people trying to stay alive. We cannot help you. We won't." She says coldly. "Leave this place before you draw someone in." I let out a sigh.

"Clearly, they don't want us here; let's go," I say to Orion, turning my back to Arkadia's voice. "I see why you didn't want to show me this…whatever it is," I add, walking away.

"Wait!" A voice shouts, making my heart sink. "Arkadia, let me pass." She hisses, her voice stern and fierce. I hold my ground, unable to move, as a soft hum fills my ears. Four feet softly land on the ground behind me. I stay still, taking a deep breath as she approaches.

"Angel, turn around…I need to see that it's you." She whispers in the sweetest tone I have ever heard her speak, her voice slightly breaking. You wouldn't be able to guess that the fierce woman only moments ago is the same person. I take another breath as I turn, our green eyes meeting. My wings go limp at the sight of her, softly brushing against the dirt. *Midnight.*

Chapter Nine

Midnight

Midnight jumps up from the cave, her ears back and frustration fueling her body. The sword is gone, and it is all her fault. She had been moving it from place to place, trying to keep it hidden from them, but the minions were everywhere nowadays. She thought it would be safe to put it in the cave now, as it had been years since she had been here.

"You should have given it to me." Arkadia snaps, annoyance filling her voice.

"And why would I do that? I would never see it again!" Midnight replies. Arkadia is a coward in her mind, doing nothing while she hides in her little sanctuary. There is a war going on, and she couldn't care less. She is determined never to fight Lucifer or his army again.

Arkadia had fought by Midnight's side many years ago in the battle where Midnight lost her love. She assumed that Arkadia had perished, but she was wrong.

"At least it wouldn't be in the hands of the devil. Come on; we should get back. They could be near; we can't cause a scene." Midnight rolls her eyes. *The world would surely end if you ever had to fight anything again.* She thinks to herself. Arkadia's motto is to stay completely invisible, which seems to have worked so far. Even Midnight thought all of the shapeshifters were dead until she met Orion. His family seemed right to leave Arkadia and her followers behind;

they could not be convinced of anything.

Once they reached the entrance to the Sanctuary, Arkadia made sure to scout the entire area before motioning for Midnight to come through. *She has got to be the most paranoid person I have ever met.* She thinks to herself, making her way toward the barrier. Passing through it was uncomfortable; she had to force herself to walk straight into trees. Her body fills with a tingling sensation as soon as she reaches them before a large clearing comes into view.

Amid the clearing, there is a small village full of primitive houses likely older than Midnight herself. It is as if she is stepping through time, back to how things used to be before this world's modernization.

"I'll leave you to it, just try not to bother anyone." Arkadia commands, her brown hair flipping as she turns around quickly.

Midnight walks toward her hut, slowly walking past a small group of children playing in the dirt. The oldest, maybe twelve, shifts into a rather large hawk before pinning his friend down playfully. Watching them fills her with joy, as she never imagined she would get to see young shifters play again. It is truly a shame that they must grow up inside a dome.

The hawk looks up at her, immediately jumping off his friend and turning back into a boy. He lowers his head before speaking. "I am sorry; it won't happen again." She tilts her head before remembering one of Arkadia's many rules: no play fighting. She believes it will give them false hope that they can fight someday. *As it should.* Midnight thinks to herself.

"Nonsense, you do not have to apologize to me. Just be glad I saw you before anyone else did." She says gently, giving them a wink before turning toward her hut.

She gently pushes through the door made of hide and makes her way to the bed, letting guilt fill her as she questions herself. *Why did you not bring the sword here? Arkadia probably would have taken it, but it would be safer here than in the devil's hands! What a fool I have been!*

After lying there for a few hours while hating on herself, Midnight approaches the dining area. It is a relatively large pavilion made of wood and stone, with a few rows of tables lined neatly underneath it. She makes herself comfortable on the far end, sitting quietly on her bench while waiting for the cooks to pass out dishes.

"Why is she still an animal?" A child softly whispers from some-where around her, followed by a hush from his parents. Midnight ig-nores this, as she has gotten used to the other shifters questioning her inability to turn back. It was somewhat overwhelming when she first arrived here, with so many young faces; they couldn't understand what she had gone through. Even some of the older members looked at her with open judgment. They had never seen the true light of day…or just how dark the world could be.

"Good evening, Dark Ones. I hope you all have had a pleasant day. Before our meal, let us thank the Lord for keeping us safe," Arka-dia speaks to the small assembly of shifters, including Midnight bow-ing their heads for the prayer. "Thank you, Father, for this meal that you have given us. Thank you for giving our hunters safety as they ventured beyond our border and for continuing to watch over us. We ask that you continue to do so, so that our community may have a chance to rebuild our once great civilization. Amen."

"Amen." Midnight whispers before eagerly digging into her fresh venison. Hers is the only uncooked one, not that she cares. The pan-ther part of her has always enjoyed raw meat. She does her best to eat humanely; the last thing she wants is to draw even more attention to herself.

Before she can finish, a strange dark feeling starts to overcome her. It is as though Lucifer himself has just gotten extremely close, filling her body with a warning. *How did he find us?* She thinks, worry and adrenaline pumping through her.

She jolts her head up, carefully scanning everyone around her. It is as though the breath has left everyone's lungs; no one is moving, and most of their faces are white as ghosts. *And these are the remain-ing shapeshifters?* She groans, thinking that all hope might indeed be lost.

Her attention goes to Arkadia, who is now standing up, a calm expression on her face. It would be impossible to tell she is worried, apart from her shaky hands.

"Everyone," She makes her voice stern. "Stay calm, and head to your homes. Coda, come with me." She commands, immediately rushing off, her second in command close to her side. Midnight watches as panic unfolds before her; it is clear most of them have never felt a threat before, let alone one this strong.

"This isn't Lucifer…" She whispers to herself. The warning inside of her feels different. It is as strong as him, if not stronger. But it is not him. This is something new, yet somehow familiar. She shakes her head in confusion before jumping off of her seat.

"Do what she says! Stop panicking and be quiet!" Midnight shouts, annoyed by the frenzy unfolding before her. Mothers carry their children with wide eyes, and older people struggle to push past people as they run. She lets out a sigh before turning toward the direction of the threat.

She creeps behind a building, beginning to hear Arkadia's voice. "I know who she is; I am not a fool. Her energy is strong. She's not welcome here. I will not have any of our blood lost for her foolish cause." *It's a she?* Midnight asks herself, slowly creeping up behind her. She vaguely hears Orion speaking. *Why won't she let him in?*

"She will expose us all," Arkadia replies to him, seeming extremely annoyed. Midnight tilts her head. *Who is she?* She tries to reach out with her mind, but the magic is too strong. Only Arkadia can reach through the barrier.

"Expose you all? Who are you?" A young woman's voice asks, sounding oddly familiar. Arkadia snaps back at her, trying to get her to leave. *Is this the thing giving off the energy? How could a young woman—*

"Clearly, they don't want us here; let's go." The girl says, her voice sounding hopeless. She is leaving. *No way.* Midnight's heart jumps. *The prophecy! How could I not see it?*

"Wait!" She frantically calls, hope filling her heart as she pushes Arkadia aside, jumping through without hesitation. Leader or not, Midnight is not about to follow her command. She nearly crashes into Orion as she comes through, who is standing just a few feet in front of her. His eyes widen as they meet hers. It had been about a year since they saw each other, but that didn't matter right now. She focuses her eyes past him, her heart dropping at the sight before her.

It is Angel, but she is much different. Her beautiful white wings are no more; they are littered with black. Some white is visible, checkered throughout them, but she is clearly full of darkness. Her body stands much taller than before; she has aged well. *Where has she been all of this time, if not dead?* Midnight thinks to herself, hating that she had gone so long thinking she was gone.

"Angel, turn around… I need to see that it's really you." Midnight whispers, trying to hide the emotion in her voice. She holds her breath as Angel's eyes meet hers. They are still their bright green, the colors dancing around in them. *It is her.* She thinks to herself, observing Angel as she lets her wings touch the ground, clearly just as overwhelmed as Midnight is. *My, what has this poor girl been through?*

Chapter Ten

The Dark Ones

"Midnight, I…" I start to say, tears swelling in my eyes. She doesn't hesitate to approach, instantly jumping onto my chest and hooking her paws around my shoulders to balance herself, her head gently pressing against mine.

"You don't have to say anything. I'm just happy to see you alive." She whispers, giving me a squeeze with her surprisingly strong cat legs. I wrap her in my wings momentarily and let the tears run down my face. *She must be so disappointed.* I think to myself, remembering the last time we saw each other. *She watched me try to kill myself. She watched me…kill him…*

After a moment, she pushes off my chest and plants her paws back on the ground. She scans my body up and down, walking in a small circle around me. I stay silent, closing my eyes and letting my head drop as she examines me. She stops in front of me again, her face holding back tears.

"Angel, I am so sorry… If I had known you were alive this whole time–"

"Shh, It's okay, Midnight. I didn't even know I was alive." I try to soothe her.

"You didn't know you were alive?" She questions, confusion filling her face. *That came out wrong.* I think to myself.

"Not really; I was in a coma. I woke up from it two months ago." I say quietly. Her eyes move to Orion.

"How did you find her?"

"She was in the meadow; I was out hunting and felt her…presence." He struggles to find the words.

"The meadow?" Midnight asks a hint of concern in her voice. "What made you go there, sweet child?" She asks me.

"It's the first place I wanted to see once I woke up. I had to see it for myself."

"Where were you when you woke up?" She asks, curiosity building in her.

"I–" I start to say.

"Sorry to interrupt this," A woman whom I could only assume to be Arkadia suddenly appears, her yellow eyes on me. *Where did she come from?* "She can't stay here, Midnight. That negative feeling she is giving off will surely draw in minions." Midnight glares at her.

"She can stay here as long as Orion and I say she can." She growls, taking a step between the two of us. "She needs our protection. The barrier will conceal her enough. Keeping her at the gate is the only real threat." *Barrier? Gate?* I question. *Why does Orion get a say?* A multitude of questions starts swimming in my mind.

"No one will like this," Arkadia scowls, her piercing eyes staring at me disgustingly. I take a step farther behind Midnight. I am unsure I want to be around such an openly hostile woman. "She is clearly damaged. I'll give you a day so I can organize a meeting." She turns around, promptly walking straight into the trees before us. In an instant, her body vanishes from sight.

"What the…" I whisper, staring at where she had been only moments ago.

"Come." Midnight commands, brushing off my surprise. "Walk directly behind me. It should grant you passage." Horrified, I walk so close to Midnight that her tail lightly brushes my body as we walk for the wall of trees in front of us. I glance back at Orion, who is slowly coming up behind me. He gives me an encouraging nod, but I am unimpressed. *How can we just walk through trees?*

As Midnight's head comes in contact with a tree, her body does not stop. Instead, she continues forward, a quiet hum filling my ears as she walks through the now shimmering barrier. I grab her tail, making her body tense slightly as we enter.

My vision blurs for a split second as my body fills with pleasant tingles, followed by a slight popping noise as I reach the other side. Midnight flicks her tail away from my hand as I turn around. *Sorry.* I think to myself. *I must have squeezed too hard.* I see Orion clear as day, walking toward the shimmering barrier, now completely visible.

"It is like the armor was," I whisper, remembering how Justin's armor shimmered ever so slightly.

"Indeed. It is from the same magic." Midnight replies from beside me. "It does not let anyone in who has a wicked heart."

"Then it is broken," I say to her, ignoring her angry glance as I focus on the new area I have walked into. It is as though I had just come upon a movie scene; about two dozen tiny homes are littered throughout a large meadow, all from materials you could find in the wild. Their walls are made of stacked stones covered in green moss; the doors are made of thick curtains of animal hide. The ceilings are all made of wood and thatch woven together. Small stone and dirt pathways lead from each house, connecting to the large and rugged path that Midnight and I currently stand on.

"How come you have never told me of this place?" I turn to her, a hint of anger in my voice.

"She did not know it existed. No one does." Arkadia pipes in, drawing my attention to the small crowd now forming behind her, all their wide eyes on me, the fear seeping off them almost too much to handle. *Why are they so afraid of me?* I question. "We have been protected since the beginning of the shapeshifters. A haven for those in need to take refuge in, away from the judgmental humans and murderous Lucifer."

"Since the beginning? Does that mean that you are all shapeshifters?" I ask, excitement filling my voice. *Exactly what we need! They can help us.*

"Settle down, child. Yes, we are all shapeshifter descendants. But we do not take part in the fighting anymore. It nearly wiped us from existence." She answers with a hint of grief in her voice. *I thought it did wipe you from existence.* I think to myself, remembering how much grief Midnight had over her lost shapeshifters. Yet, here we are, standing in front of a whole village of them.

"Lucifer will wipe everyone from existence if we don't do anything," I reply to her, my excitement turning to anger.

'Now is not the time Angel.' Midnight reaches into my mind and

gives me a gentle nudge.

"That is highly unlikely; we are completely safe here," Arkadia says calmly, gazing at the crowd. "I am sure most of you are aware by her looks that this girl standing before us is Angel, who has been prophesied about. It is true; she can shift into any animal she wants, even a dragon," A few gasps escape from them. "She is *only* here to hide. Do not bombard her; let her rest." She finishes up, gesturing with her hands for the crowd to disperse.

"Try not to draw too much attention to yourself. It's the last thing we need right now." Arkadia says to me. "As for you, Midnight, why don't you show her and Orion around. I have a couple of empty huts across from yours." Midnight nods to her before walking down the path in front of us.

I look back toward Orion, who seems hesitant to explore. He takes a deep breath before jogging up to my side.

"Your horses will be fine. They know how to open their stalls, right? And there's plenty of hay in the–"

"It's not that." He cuts me off. "I just…I did not expect her to let me come in as well. I shouldn't be here."

"Why not? This place seems safe enough… I mean, we just walked through a barrier! Who knew those were even real!" I say rather excitedly, trying to improve his mood.

"I know it's safe. I just don't want people to realize who I am…"

"Why would that even matter?"

He takes a deep breath. "No one knew my parents had–" Midnight turns around, interrupting him. We stopped before a pavilion made from logs and stone, standing tall above an array of handmade tables and chairs. *Right. He was hiding on a farm under a different name when we met.* I curiously wonder why that would matter here of all places.

"This is the dining area. Meals are served twice a day here, breakfast and dinner. Usually, about twice a month, we have community meetings. It is not very exciting." Midnight explains. "This is the center of the village; my hut is pretty close, right down the path over there," she gestures to a small dirt path winding from the main one, houses littered on both sides. "And past the pavilion, there is the meeting place for the leaders, followed by Arkadia's home. But it's best not to go over there. She doesn't like visitors." She scowls, seeming to be speaking from experience.

The hill behind the pavilion blocked our view, concealing the meeting place Midnight spoke of. My eyes linger on it for a moment. *If I could get Arkadia alone… maybe I could talk some sense into her. Surely, she isn't that blind…*

Midnight clears her throat, followed by a slight shake of her head. She motions for us to continue, leading us down the side trail to her hut. It is a relatively short walk; we only pass by three homes before stopping in front of one of them. Midnight gently pushes the hide door up as she walks through before disappearing behind it. I hesitantly grab it, pushing it to the side as I slide behind her.

The hut is definitely an upgrade from her previous home. Rather than a bed made of grass and moss, a soft mattress lay on the floor with a fuzzy brown blanket. The floor is covered in animal pelts, all appearing to be some type of deer. A small wooden table with two chairs sits opposite the bed, next to a small window covered with yet another pelt.

I sit on one of the chairs, prompting Orion to do the same.

"Oh no, you don't. You need to rest, both of you. The two huts directly across from me are vacant. They should have beds." She objects.

"What? We have too much to talk about. There's so much I need to–"

"Hush, child. We will talk in the morning. Now go, don't make me tell you again." She growls. I let out a sigh. *This is how I get greeted after all these years? It's good to know how much she missed me.*

"If I leave, will you promise to get Arkadia to speak to me? Alone?" I ask. Midnight flattens her ears.

"Even if I did, it would do nothing. Trust me. Now go." Her voice becomes deep, a hint of anger starting to rise. I try to step toward her, but Orion's arm blocks my path as he pulls me toward the door. I let out a huff as he pulls me through.

"It's been years since I have seen her. Yet she won't stay up to talk." I sigh, giving in to his pull toward the other two huts.

"You have plenty of time to do that. Just listen to her and get some rest. Which one do you want?"

"I don't care," I reply coldly, disappointment fueling me.

"How about the left, then? I'll take the other." He replies, clearly annoyed. I ignore this and make my way into my hut. It is nearly identical to Midnight's, the only furniture being a bed and a table. I let my body fall flat onto the bed, sighing as I buried my face in the firm mattress.

Chapter Eleven

Hope

The following day, I am woken by a young girl who can't be older than ten. She is a small thing with short black hair that is so shiny it almost glows. Her green eyes are bright with life, sneaking glances at my wings as she offers me a small salad.

"Thank you…" I try to ask for her name.

"Nymeria and you're welcome. Feel free to eat here or in the pavilion. Have a blessed day." She chirps, returning to her small tray of salads. She left as quickly as she came without another word.

After gulping down my egg salad, I eagerly walk toward Midnight's hut. There is still so much I want to say to her, so much more we must discuss. I have so many questions, and I am sure she does too. Despite the massive forest surrounding us, the sun shines brightly on me as I go. *This sure is a strange place.* I think to myself as I reach her hut.

Disappointment fills me as I notice her pelt door rolled up, revealing a space beside a dirty plate on the table. I let out a sigh before turning my attention toward the village. She has to be somewhere around here; it isn't very big.

Walking toward the main path, I notice a surprising variety of people around me. The village is starting to come to life, everyone waking up and going about their days. Most of them avoid looking in my direction, likely from the energy everyone says I am giving off. I remain hopeful, giving those who look my way cheerful smiles that leave them turning around. *I'm just trying to be friendly.* I think to myself, annoyance rising within me.

Children run about the street before me, laughing and giggling as they play. My heart warms as I watch, filling me with memories of running through the woods with Justin. *Is this world all they have known?* I wonder how strict Arkadia is.

One of them trips and falls, prompting me to make my way over to her. I realize it is the same girl that had given me breakfast only minutes ago. She instantly transforms into a yellow bird-like creature, jumping into the air and taking flight. She has the head of an eagle but the body of a lion—a *griffin.* I stand in awe, watching as she turns around and dives at the other child, who has shifted into a giant snake. He flashes his fangs at her with a playful hiss just before they collide, rolling away in a giggling mass.

I watch in amusement as the snake wraps around the griffin, trying to hold on as she runs around the ground and lets out low growls.

"Nymeria, Monica!" A stern male voice calls. "Don't rough house so much; you know it's against the rules to shift like that!" He warns them, his green eyes meeting mine for a moment. "Stay away from the kids." He says rather coldly.

"I wasn't–" Midnight appears, jogging up to my side, her eyes flat as she approaches the angry man.

"Leave her be, Coda. She has never seen shifting children before. Angel, come." She says, dismissing him with a quick flick of her tail. *They're not allowed to play. Just how closed off is this place?* I question myself, anger rising within me.

"You two are going to get us killed." He whispers under his breath. Midnight's ear twitches, but she keeps walking.

"What's his problem?" I ask her once we are out of earshot.

"You." She replies rather confidently. I let out a snort. "I'm serious; this place is different, Angel. Protected, no need for fighting. They know the history, that you are the one that was prophesied. Your being here is a sign of death, especially with that dark feeling you're emitting. You are made to fight."

"Are they protected, though? Is hiding in a bubble really living?" I challenge, gesturing to the dome around us.

"It's all some of these people know. Their life before this was… complicated. Lucifer doesn't know they exist, and they want to keep it that way."

"So they'll just hide here and never teach their children how to protect themselves? Not allowing them even to play fight? It doesn't make sense. It's… selfish." I reply, my mind going to the woman in the gas station. "Haven't you seen it out there?"

"Of course I have. I was out there most of this time. Trying to hide the swo… I mean, trying to hide myself. Those minions are brave without you around." I stop in my tracks.

"You were trying to hide the sword? You had it?" I ask her, her nervous eyes meeting mine.

"Past tense, yes. I didn't want to worry you about it. We can get it back." She says with a small amount of hope in her voice. I shake my head at her.

"I think it's time I tell you what happened to me and how I got here," I say sternly, making her ears perk up.

"Alright, let's go back into my hut then." She agrees, promptly turning herself around. We take about two steps before Arkadia comes into view, giving us a look that doesn't seem too pleased. Midnight stops beside me, watching Arkadia closely as she approaches.

Arkadia is an intimidating woman. Her slim yet muscular body proudly moves as she walks, clearly showing her top-ranking status among the people here. I haven't seen many leaders, but she fits the bill. She wears leather clothes, with a small gap between her tight pants and top that shows her belly button. She appears to be in her thirties, but it is hard to tell.

"Good morning. I hope you are well rested?" Arkadia asks, her piercing yellow eyes on me.

"Well enough," I reply.

"Good. We will meet at around noon in the building behind the pavilion. Midnight is welcome as well." She turns to leave.

"What about Orion?" I ask her, realizing I have yet to see him today. She raises an eyebrow.

"He left, did he not? Either way, he is not needed for this. I will see you in a bit." She turns again, hurrying toward a group of people in the distance.

"Did you know he left?" I ask Midnight, a hint of sorrow in my voice.

"Yes, he left early this morning. Something about his horses." I let out a relieved sigh. *Of course.* "Now, we best hurry. You need to catch me up on everything that has happened before this meeting."

Once we are safely back inside the hut, I begin the story by explaining my strange dream before I woke up. She seems rather interested in it, especially since my mind seems to have created the people I saw, something that shouldn't be possible. Her reaction makes me yet again question whether or not it was real. I continue to talk about how I found the sword lying beside me, safely in its sheath, and how I managed to slice a man open with it.

"You killed someone with it?" Midnight gasps, her eyes widening in an instant. "What happened once you did? What did you feel?" I tilt my head. *Why does she care so much?*

"Nothing, really. I was just surprised by how easily it cut through him. It seemed rather happy about it; it let out a little 'hum' right after. I felt a little energized after, but nothing crazy." I answer, remembering how I did seem to get extra energy after the kill.

"Really? That is incredible..." Midnight trails off, clearly deep in thought. *I thought she knew everything about it.* I think to myself. After a few moments of silence, she continues. "Usually, to be able to wield it, you have to take the oath. Not to mention, the sword was designed to kill you if you were to become corrupt. So how would it allow you to use it... Where is it now?" She breaks her train of thought, seeming to be confused.

"Safe," I whisper, tuning in my ears to ensure no one is nearby. "At Orion's farm, in a hidden location." Midnight's nostrils flare as she thinks for a moment.

"Call it." She commands. "I need to test something."

"Call it here? What makes you think I can–"

"Just focus. Think of the sword and its sheath. Hold up your hand and say, 'I summon you.'. If you believe it will come, it should. You made a kill with it, so it should be bonded to you now." I take a deep breath, trying to take in her words. Would I be able to summon it if I shouldn't even hold it in the first place? *None of this makes sense.* I think to myself.

Discouraged, I slowly lift my hand and close my eyes. An image of the sword, lying safely in a tack box inside the barn, wrapped in a horse blanket, comes to mind. I picture its shining emerald, how it glows ever so slightly. The same green tint that is within my own eyes. *Talk about a coincidence… Okay, focus.* I take a deep breath and open my fingers slightly.

"I summon you!" I shout, my body staggering backward as a force strikes my hand with a loud crack and a flash so bright, I see it with my eyes closed. My fingers close around the leather sheath as I take in the force I was just hit with.

"How extraordinary…" Midnight whispers, prompting me to open my eyes for the first time. Sure enough, the sword, still in its sheath, is now resting in my hand. How this is even possible is beyond my comprehension, yet here it is. "It would be best to keep it with you from now on." She suggests, her eyes still lingering on it. I slowly pull it from the sheath, admiring the blade's beauty—a weapon crafted by God himself in my hands. *I got too comfortable there.* I think to myself, remembering how careless I became with the sword while I was with Orion.

"It used to terrify me. Now… it holds so many memories… so much value." I say to her, eyeing the blade carefully. "I want nothing more than to protect it. It was his, the only piece I have left." I choke, memories of Justin coming to mind once more.

Midnight's eyes flicker with regret before it disappears into seriousness once more. "Angel, there is something I should tell you, but I have no idea how." She confesses, trying her best to read my expression.

I take a deep breath, reaching out for her paw. "Just say it; it can't make me feel any worse than I already do." I encourage her, bracing myself.

"Well, I don't think that the—" Midnight gets cut off by commotion outside.

"What in God's name just happened?" Arkadia's voice shouts. Midnight frowns before turning her head toward the door. *How many times is this woman going to interrupt us?* I roll my eyes as she approaches.

"Nothing of concern; we were just getting ready for the meeting." Arkadia's head pops through the pelt, her eyes instantly locking on the sword. *This can't be good.*

"I thought Lucifer had it? And how on Earth is Angel holding it? Did she… summon it? She shouldn't be able to… neither of you should…" She trails off, her eyes going to the ground for a moment. "Just try not to draw any more attention, please. You're already all this place is talking about. We will expect you both in the meeting place in an hour." She says firmly, a hint of uneasiness in her voice.

"Alright," Midnight turns back to me. "Continue with the story. What happened after you killed the minion?"

Chapter Twelve

Sacrifice

The meeting place is nestled near Arkadia's hut, surrounded by a large field. The meeting place is roughly the size of four small huts. It is a circular building made of the same materials as the others. A chimney with a constant stream of gray smoke sticks out from the very middle of the roof. Midnight tells me that whenever the fire is lit, it means a meeting is or is about to take place. The building door is made of two large purple sheets and made of silk, both of which are rolled up and tied in front of a wide opening.

Midnight and I slowly make our way toward it, walking side by side. Part of me can't help but feel like I am about to be put on trial; there is no way Arkadia will let me stay here much longer, so I have to make the most of it.

"This strangely reminds me of when I was on trial as a kid," I whisper to Midnight as we walk, making Midnight's seriousness cave into a small smile as she fights a laugh. It quickly dissipates as we reach the entrance, replaced by her usual stone-cold expression.

"Be on top of yourself in here, no jokes." She commands. I nod my head in agreement, noticing the guards before us. There is no room for error now. The guards are two shirtless men that appear to be twins, their dark skin littered with scars. They both have long black hair tied back in tight ponytails. Despite their rugged appearances, their smiles are welcoming.

The room is completely open, with a large campfire in the center. Benches covered in various animal hides and pelts litter the surrounding area. Directly across from the entrance, Arkadia sits atop a large chair slightly elevated above the rest. Her hair is tied back into one long braid, gently resting on her shoulder.

About half of the twenty seats inside the hut are filled with men and women, all of whom have their eyes locked on Midnight and me. Arkadia stands at the sight of us, prompting the others to do the same.

"Welcome, Midnight, Angel." Arkadia carries her voice across the room. "Please, join us." Her voice softens as she gestures toward the seating. I let Midnight lead the way as she walks in front of me, sitting down beside one of the benches near an elderly woman. I take my place next to her, letting my wings relax as I sit.

"Now, I want to introduce you to our tribe leaders and elders. Everyone in this room is part of a shapeshifting family, aging back thousands of years. There are three main ones: those of the land, those of the sky, and those of fire. I am sure you are quite familiar with the fire ones," She explains. My mind shifts to Lucifer and his minions. *Are all of the fire ones bad?* I question. *And are there no water shapeshifters?* I repeat her words: land, sky, and fire.

"Each family tended to favor one type of animal over the years, and the tribes continued to split off into a wide variety that we have today. In this room alone, there are seven different types of shifters." My eyes widen as I scan the room momentarily, looking eagerly at the people before me. "Yes, it is quite amazing. Now, I want to open the floor to any elder who wishes to speak to her first." Arkadia gestures to the crowd. I swallowed hard; I didn't realize that people other than her would speak to us.

"Well, I think I should address the elephant in the room," A man stands, looking no older than fifty. "How is it that she was able to summon the sword? Wasn't it written that no shapeshifter can hold it?" His dark green eyes meet mine, flicking down for a moment to catch a glimpse of the sheath. I slide a hand onto the sword's hilt, a protective feeling overcoming me. *There had to be a reason why Midnight didn't keep it here.*

"We don't really know, truthfully." Midnight speaks up. "It saved her when she woke up from that coma. She was able to defend herself despite being so weak." I nod in agreement, remembering how tired I felt that day.

"It still doesn't make sense to me." He replies, eyeing me carefully. "Did you make a kill with it?"

"Yes," I say quietly, causing a few gasps around the room. The man's eyes widen, and he puts his hand on his chin as he thinks.

"Fascinating. I suppose the prophecies can only tell us so much." *Prophesies. How many are there?* I question, remembering how Midnight said I had been prophesied about.

"Does anyone else have anything to ask?" Arkadia speaks, her eyes scanning the room.

This time, an elderly woman stands. Her silvery hair was braided behind her head, reaching just above her hips. Her eyes seem to be filled with curiosity as they gaze into mine. I give her a shy smile as I straighten myself up.

"Angel, we have all heard some hard-to-believe tales about you in recent years. In fact, most of us thought you had been dead this whole time. Some even suggested you never existed at all," Her eyes shifted to a woman in the corner for a moment. "But, looking at you now, it is clear that everything had some truth to it. Tell me, what do you believe your purpose to be?" Her words make me pause for a moment, thinking back on what Midnight had said to me all those years ago. *To kill the devil.* But that was only part of it, right?

"I ask myself that all the time. I know I was created to destroy Lucifer, but I can't help but think that's not all of it. I think I am meant to protect the wellbeing of the humans as well." The woman gives me a gentle nod before sitting back down.

'You're doing great.' Midnight reaches my mind, filling me with encouragement.

"Now, if no one else has a question, I would like to ask one of my own." Arkadia's eyes meet mine. I tightly grip my pant leg in preparation.

"Do you know why your eyes are green? Or why, when you shifted for the first time, why green swirled around you?" I shake my head at her. She pauses for a moment before continuing. "You'll notice the world around us. The trees, the grass, the infinite number of plants. They are all life, and from them stems everything else," she stretches her arms out, gesturing into the sky. "As shapeshifters, we were created to protect that life, so it is only fitting that our magic should be green. God made it this way." She says confidently.

'Am I allowed to speak?' I ask Midnight. She nods her head ever so slightly, her gaze never leaving Arkadia.

"I have never heard it laid out that way before…it makes me feel a bit more connected. But something stands out to me," I hesitate, not wanting to overstep my boundaries. *You've come this far.*

"Go on, what is it?" Arkadia asks.

"Well, if God created us to protect life, why are you not out there defending the humans?" Arkadia shifts in her chair, seeming slightly annoyed as the others turn their heads toward her. She takes a deep breath before bringing her hands together in her lap.

"Angel, look around you. This is it. There are fifteen people in this room, including the two of you. We are the only shapeshifters left that know how to fight. We are not enough. We must continue to hide and grow our community, preserve it, so one day we may fight."

"So, you would rather sit here and do nothing while humans are slaughtered daily? Have you been outside? By the time you're ready, whatever that means, everyone will be dead." I scoff. Arkadia's eyes flicker with anger.

"We must preserve ourselves; I will not have innocent blood shed."

"It's being shed every day!" I raise my voice, making Midnight stir beside me.

"We are not ready. You must watch yourself, *child*. You do not understand what is at stake here."

"Not ready? I stood against Lucifer and an entire army, with nothing but a human and two other shifters by my side. Imagine how much more we can do with even just one more!" Arkadia jumps to her feet with her fists clenched into tight balls.

"Enough of this. You two are no longer welcome here." She hisses, gesturing for us to leave. Midnight stands, her ears pinned back.

"I hope you will get rid of this blindness soon enough, Arkadia. I wish you well." She says quietly, fighting back evident anger. She turns around and walks off, flicking her tail for me to follow. I look toward the elders and gently bow before turning around and hurrying after her.

Midnight stays completely silent as we go, walking with high and proud steps as the rest of the village watches as we leave. I place my hand on her shoulder, following her lead and holding my wings high.

"We tried," I whisper. "I hope it was enough."

"It was. You'll see." She says confidently.

We walk through the village silently as Arkadia's men follow us from a distance, watching us closely. Midnight doesn't look back as she walks through the barrier before me. I hesitate momentarily, remembering how strange it felt the first time. I stare carefully at the shimmering wall before me, knowing I will likely never see the inside of this place again. *What is wrong with me? I lost my cool so easily.* I scold myself, feeling the hope drain from my body. I close my eyes for a moment before stepping through.

The familiar tingles surge through my body once more as I go, followed by a soft pop as I reach the other side. I sigh in relief as I look into the forest around me, cool air filling my lungs. The forest has always been calming, welcoming me as an old friend. Even though the Sanctuary is surrounded by it, something within the barrier keeps out the real forest feel.

I turn my attention to Midnight, who also seems to enjoy the fresh air around us. She sits quietly, her head raised into the air, her eyes closed, and her black lips curled into a slight smile. *She is so calm about all of this.* I think to myself. I might have just blown our chances of having real help against Lucifer, yet here she is with a smile.

"Now what?" I ask her.

"We wait." She replies gently, continuing to enjoy the fresh air.

"For what?"

"As I said before, you will see. We did not do all of that for nothing, Angel. Just relax for a moment. You have earned it." I sigh as I let my body sit on the ground somewhat hard, creating a soft "thud noise" that makes Midnight's ear twitch. How could she expect me to sit and wait after what happened?

After a few minutes of silence, I stand up and pace. I wanted to distance myself from that unbending woman and her followers.

"Could you stop that?" Midnight groans.

"We can't just sit here. We must go out and do…something." I protest, continuing to walk back and forth on my patch of dirt.

"And we will," She replies, her eyes on the tree barrier before us. I follow her gaze, noticing a tiny flicker.

"What's happening?" I ask her, watching a man jump out of the barrier, immediately turning around as if he were being followed. I take a few steps back, only for Midnight to walk toward him with joy in her eyes.

"Luke, I hope you have good news?" She asks him. He turns toward us, seeming to be full of nerves.

"You could say that. You two caused quite the spectacle; I will give you that. Arkadia is dealing with a lot of confused civilians. And some of them are calling for us to start training!"

"Really?" I raise an eyebrow, disbelief in my voice.

"Yes, just a couple, though. But it is something. I am sure the people will be more willing within a few months. It will be a process." *Months? How can we wait that long...It has been long enough.*

"Good. Hopefully, the buzz keeps up. Let the others know that Angel and I will go out and kill every minion in our path, searching for more shifters. For anyone who can help us. We have a lot of work to do, but we will no longer be quiet." Midnight replies, a fire building within her. Luke gives her a slight nod before disappearing back into the barrier.

"I don't understand. What is that supposed to do?"

"Start an uprising of sorts. We need Arkadia on our side, and ruffling her people's feathers might be a good way to nudge her in the right direction."

"Are you sure? It sounds more like a good way to make her never want to speak to us again." I reply, discouragement rising within me. Arkadia did not seem like the type of person to change easily.

"You don't know her like I do, Angel. She cares deeply for her people. If enough want a change, she will give it to them." Midnight replies rather confidently.

Chapter Thirteen

The Search Begins

We decide to go to Orion's farm once we leave, hopeful that he is still tending to his animals. Since we are about to embark on some impossible quest, he deserves to know. We want to tell him our plan without expecting him to come. He has already been through so much.

The walk to the farm is relatively quiet, as Midnight and I both seem lost in our thoughts. I can't help but regret how rashly I acted back there, giving us a one-way ticket out of the Sanctuary. Still, Midnight seems hopeful. She already has a plan, whatever that may be. I wish she would be more open to me about it, as it has every bit to do with me as it does with her. I know Midnight is not the best at communicating, but I figure after all this time, she would trust me a little more. I am not the child I once was; she must see that.

"Midnight, do you remember right before Arkadia interrupted us? You said you had something to tell me." I break the silence, hoping to ease her into discussing her plans.

She lets out a long sigh. "I don't think now is the time. Be patient, please. Look, we are almost there." She answers, gesturing toward the outskirts of the farm.

"Will you tell me your plan, then?" I ask.

"Let's just see if Orion is here first." She answers. I sigh as we approach, focusing on what lies in front of me. All the pastures are empty, including the goat and chicken pens. The usual noise of the farm is gone, filled with the sounds of distant birds chirping around us. Panicked, I shift my eyes to the barn with its open doors. *Please be okay.* I think to myself as my walk turns to a run.

The stalls inside the barn are empty; all their doors unlatched— hay and crumbs of grain litter the aisleway, which is usually very well kept. I make my way to the hay pile, only to find it empty. *Where are you?* I question, setting my gaze upon the house.

Midnight gives me a worried look as I bolt toward the house, nearly breaking the door off its hinges as I open it. "Orion, where are you?" I call out to him. Hearing nothing in return, I walk inside. The house is an entirely different scene. Everything appears to be the same, clean and as it should be. With a relieved sigh, I approach his room, hoping for a clue.

I hesitate momentarily in front of his door, realizing I have never been inside. Surely he wouldn't mind, though; his life may be at stake. I slowly creak it open to reveal one of the cleanest rooms I have ever seen. His floor is made of a soft white carpet that looks almost too clean, apart from the dirty footprints I created. The room is well-kept and organized, with everything having its own little spot. The only thing different is the large wooden desk in the corner. It is littered with papers and various pens and pencils.

Curiosity driving me, I walk toward it and open a hardback sketchbook. Warmth fills my cheeks for a moment as I notice the first page, a drawing of me as a cheetah, staring into the forest with my wings spread and my head high. The amount of detail is astonishing, everything from the trees to each individual hair on my fur. *You never told me you're an artist.* I think to myself, continuing to flip through the pages. It contains various animal and scenery drawings, primarily horses and wolves. An oddly familiar illustration makes my heart skip as I see it. It is two wolves by a creek, leaning down to take a drink. Their similarity to Orion makes me think about the first time we ran through the woods together. That seemed like a lifetime ago now.

"Find anything?" Midnight's voice breaks my concentration, causing me to jump away from the book and close it with a bang. *And I thought I was supposed to have good senses.* I criticize myself, meeting her gaze.

"Not really..." I say, ignoring her lingering eyes. "His animals are gone, and it seems like he is too. Where would he even go, especially with a herd of horses?"

"I don't think he's leaving forever, look." Midnight points her nose toward the bed, which has a stuffed backpack. I immediately move over to it, embarrassed that I missed something like that.

"Should we wait for him? Maybe he will come back for it." I say, hope filling my voice. Still, I don't understand why he would move all his animals in such a rush.

"It couldn't hurt. Hopefully, he will be back soon." She replies gently.

"Now that we are waiting, how about telling me the plan?" I suggest, prompting Midnight to give me an annoyed glance before turning toward an oversized bean bag chair. She jumps onto it, doing a couple of circles before lying down.

"It depends on how you're feeling," She stretches her paws out, seeming to enjoy the cushion. "Lucifer's minions are doing as they please, right?" I nod at her. "I am sure they are all on edge since you escaped but still taking advantage of your absence."

"Which is something we refuse to let continue," I say to her, a sense of determination rising in my chest. She nods slightly.

"So, we must stomp down hard on that freedom they feel. Have you out there and cutting them down, one by one. They'll notice, and so will the humans. The world doesn't even know you're alive. And if you're ready, it is time to make it known. Give them hope and terrify Lucifer's minions at the same time."

"You mean, expose me?" I reply, a small amount of nerves rising in my chest. My mind drifts to Leah, who thought it would be wise to do so eventually. I wonder if she is still alive…not that it matters, I have bigger things to worry about. I have spent the entirety of my life hiding, mostly due to the same person now telling me to do the opposite. *Oh, how times have changed.*

"Yes. But we will be smart about it. It will mean a lot of traveling and many nights on the run. We will be loud and fast and hopefully run into more shapeshifters. After seeing that there are about fifty in one place, I don't think it would be illogical to search for more." Her words cause my heartbeat to echo through my ears, fueling me with anxiousness. I clench my fists, thinking hard about what this could mean.

"Wouldn't this cause Lucifer to come to the open himself and give us a repeat of what has happened already?" I swallow hard. There is no way I can handle a repeat of Justin. I wasn't in control of my body, and the thought of going through that again was terrifying.

Midnight stays silent for a moment, pondering the question. She narrows her eyes before giving a slight nod as she concludes.

"I don't think so. He's smart; he knows you're much stronger now. Besides, when he does eventually show himself, we will be ready. And we won't be alone, Lord willing." She answers, confident in her answer.

"No, you won't be." Orion's voice makes us both jump to our feet. He is standing in the doorway, his posture high and strong. Although his face seems determined, a hint of sorrow lingers in his eyes. *Does he know what we are about to do?*

"I figured Arkadia wouldn't let you stay there long… so I gave my animals to an old friend. He lives a few miles from here." *Why would he give his animals away?* I question, trying to read his expression. *The backpack. He wishes to come with us!* I conclude, a flutter of excitement in my chest. The look in his eyes makes it vanish in an instant.

He has to leave everything behind. My heart aches for him, trying to imagine how hard that trip must have been. I take a few steps in his direction, touching his shoulder. He takes a step back, giving his shoulders a slight shake.

"It's okay. I'm fine," His eyes shift from me to Midnight, then back again. "I want you two to know that whatever you're planning, I am all for it. I will follow you. You have my word."

"Thank you," I gently say as he grabs his bag and straps it to his back. He looks at me carefully before grabbing another one out of his closet. Midnight seems surprised at him; her eyes are full of pride. She must see the growth as much as I do. Although, it is hard to feel happy that he is about to make a sacrifice for us.

"Do you think you could carry a backpack?" He holds the bag out toward me. I tilt my head at him, stretching my wings into the air.

"No, my wings wouldn't fit. Besides, it will be too much of a hassle." There is no way I will worry about a backpack the entire time.

"Okay. Well, I think I have enough supplies for us all in here. So long as we keep resupplying when we can." He says, placing the bag back into the closet. He scans the room for a moment, his eyes glistening with wetness. "Until next time." He whispers, turning back toward the door. He doesn't say another word as we go outside, away from the only home he's ever known. Part of me hoped he would be back here soon enough, but deep down, we all knew that would never happen. Orion has dealt with more than I can imagine these past few years, but nothing could prepare him for what we will do.

Chapter Fourteen

The Town

Midnight makes it clear that the best places for us to be are the most crowded places. The minions favor going to the more populated areas, ignoring the small towns and villages. My mind thinks of Florida, the woman hiding inside her store. It seems impossible to reach there without flying, and I know Midnight would be against me carrying her. So, we are stuck venturing through the forest on foot.

"Are we nearing anything?" I ask her, looking hopelessly at the vast forest ahead of us.

"Yes, I believe there's a relatively large town in about ten miles. You could fly up and check for us, see how close we are." She suggests, looking up toward the sky. I follow her gaze, looking longingly at the clear sky with no clouds. I haven't flown since I ran into Orion, as it felt like too significant a risk. Midnight gently nudges my side, causing my gaze to fall back on her. "Remember, we want you to be seen. Don't worry about hiding anymore."

I want to be seen. I tell myself, taking a deep breath. I have spent my whole life hiding, so the thought of openly putting myself out there feels alien. I don't know if I am ready for this, but I must be— no *more hiding*.

"Alright," I reply, taking a few steps away from her as I change into my beloved cheetah form. I stretch my wings as I look toward

Orion, who gives me an encouraging smile. I return it as energy surges through me, filling me with delight as I leap toward the sky. My body instantly relaxes as the wind brushes against my wings, lifting me effortlessly through the air.

I keep myself about one hundred feet above the treetops, hoping to get a good view of our surroundings. The forest stretches around us like a never-ending sea of trees. It's no wonder how the Sanctuary has stayed hidden for so long. I focus my attention directly ahead, hoping to catch a glimpse of the town Midnight had been talking about. *Nothing.* I sigh before focusing my energy on my wings, giving them as much power as possible.

As my energy transfers to my wings, I fly as quickly as possible, determined to find this supposed town. The forest begins to thin within a few seconds, a paved road catching my attention. I lower myself, flying directly over the winding road as it goes through a few hills and back into a flatland.

My heart jumps with excitement as a town comes into view, buildings littered throughout a relatively large area. *Civilization.* I think to myself, letting out a sigh of relief. Without much thought, I continue to fly toward it, looking for any signs of movement.

The streets and buildings are run down; most buildings have broken windows. A few scorch marks litter the sidewalks, making my stomach twist at the thought of what they were aimed at. I land softly on the pavement, bringing my wings close to my sides as I walk down the street.

'I found the town, but it looks deserted.' I reach out to Midnight. Her presence reaches my mind after a few seconds.

'What do you see?'

'Broken glass...empty cars, burnt concrete...'

'Do you feel anything? Reach out with your mind.'

I close my eyes and let my mind expand, searching for anyone else's thoughts. Emptiness fills me.

'There's nothing. No one is here.'

'Try harder than that.' Midnight commands, seeming to feel my lack of hope. I stand completely still, continuing my search. My mind focuses on everything around me, feeling for anything with life. A faint feeling reaches me, almost unnoticeable. I reach toward it, trying to figure out which way to go.

I tilt my head toward the ground, staring intently at the concrete as I concentrate. The feeling grows; the thoughts of several individuals fill me. *Are they underground?* I ask myself, unsure of how to find them. As if an answer to my question, light footsteps across the cement draw my attention.

I snap my head toward their direction, eyeing an abandoned bar carefully. A man's head barely peeks through a boarded window, his brown eyes meeting mine. I hold my ground, hoping I don't scare him off.

"Are you alone?" I call out to him. He shrinks back from the window, seeming surprised at the sound of my voice. "I'm not here to hurt anyone. I am looking for survivors. I can help you." I continue to speak, making my voice as gentle as possible.

"How do we know you're not with the dragons?" My ears go back.

"You'll have to trust my word. I am not here with them. I am here to stop them."

"We don't trust anyone." He replies, his voice slightly shaken. I take a few steps to the side, my head looking up toward the sky.

"Do they come here often? Is that why you're underground?"

"Sometimes. We don't take any chances."

"I understand," I say softly, scanning the town around me. I circle once more before stopping in front of the bar. I turn myself into my human form and extend my arms out slightly. "Do I look like someone who works with the dragons?" The man remains silent, his wide eyes watching me closely. I place a hand on the hilt of the sword and pull it out. "This weapon here can chop those dragons' wings clean off. And it has. It can cut through me as well, just like butter. I intend to kill Lucifer and all his minions along with him."

The sound of a few locks unlatching makes me slide the sword back into its sheath, keeping my eyes on the door. It slowly creaks open, a tall man with dirty blonde hair peeking his head through. His face is full of curiosity and hope, but fear is holding him back.

I slowly raise my hand, placing it on my chest. I keep my eyes on him, determined to win his trust. I am sure that we can help each other.

"I am Angel—the only one of my kind. You may remember seeing me on the news while fighting the dragon on the road. I can shapeshift into any animal imaginable, including a dragon. I was created to kill Lucifer, which is exactly what I will do." I say confidently, trying to show him my sincerity.

"You're supposed to be dead… and your wings, they were white."

"Watching someone you grew up with die changes people," I reply coldly. "But I assure you, I am the same person I was."

"Okay. But I don't think we can let you in here. It's too risk—" He gets cut off by a screech from above. I immediately look into the air, watching a dark green dragon soar over us. Its dark eyes on me. The door to the bar slams shut.

I shift into my dragon form, letting out an angry roar as I follow my opponent into the sky. *Finally,* I think, almost excited to show Lucifer I am done hiding. The dragon spins around, its eyes widening at the sight of me almost upon them. I lower my head slightly, bashing into the minion's chest. It lets out a cry and falls slightly.

Taking advantage of this, I swing myself around and kick hard with my legs, sending them plummeting toward the road below. I dive after them, landing firmly on their back as they make contact. I latch my jaws around the back of its neck, using my body to keep it held down as warm blood fills my mouth. Wanting to end this as soon as possible, I swing my body around to flip theirs, exposing their belly. My claws sink into their scales as I momentarily release my jaws to bite into their throat. With a loud crunch, its body goes completely limp. I release my grip and wipe my mouth with my wing.

As I crawl off the dragon's body, I notice the man slowly approaching with disbelief in his eyes. I turn my attention toward him, giving a gentle nod to show I mean no harm. He hesitantly places a hand on the dead minion, taking a deep breath. He looks up at me after a moment, amazement filling his eyes.

"You really are here to save us, aren't you?" I lower my head so we are at eye level, causing him to take a fearful step back. My lips curl into a soft smile.

"That's all I want to do."

Chapter Fifteen

Underground

"This is remarkable!" Orion says excitedly as we descend on the elevator. It had taken Midnight and him about an hour to reach the town after I did, despite running as fast as they could. They were rather excited about it after hearing that people were hiding underneath.

I learned that the name of the man I had met earlier was Jason, and he was one of the scouts for the town. They all take turns watching from above, seeing if the coast is clear or if any other people wander their way seeking shelter. They use radio broadcasts to let others know where they are and that they have plenty of room for more.

"I wouldn't say that," Midnight replied, clearly unamused at being cramped in an elevator with us. She doesn't seem to admire anything that is man-made. The structure appears to be older than all of us, but if the humans use it a lot, that's good enough for me. Besides, even if we did fall, it's not like it can kill any of us.

"Cheer up. I am just glad they let us in here." I say happily as the elevator comes to an abrupt stop. The doors open slowly with a few groan-like creeks, revealing a small group with ashen faces. Their eyes widen at seeing us, but they hold their ground as we slowly walk out.

I spread my wings out slightly, standing tall as I walked toward them. Midnight stays close to my side, eyeing the humans carefully. They seem somewhat fearful of our presence, keeping a safe distance from our little group. Orion gives them gentle smiles, being the only human-looking one among us. *Hopefully, he can put them at ease.* I think to myself.

Jason, the one I met earlier, emerges from the crowd with a warm smile. He holds a shaking hand out to us, gesturing as he speaks. "This is Angel and her companions…" He trails off.

"Midnight," I gesture toward her. "And Orion."

"Right. Midnight and Orion. She is welcome here, as are they. I watched her kill a dragon with my own eyes right outside our entrance." A few gasps escape the crowd, followed by looks of disbelief. "She is here to help. In fact, we might be able to use her to lure in some people in need." He says happily, giving me a welcoming look. The people in front of us start chatting with one another, their voices as quiet as they can be. Not that it mattered; I could hear them clear as day.

"Where is your radio? Perhaps we can try to send a message to anyone who can hear it." Midnight suggests, not seeming to want to be around the crowd. *Always so straight to the point.* I think to myself. Marcus nods, gesturing for us to follow him. The crowd splits as we walk, making us a path deeper into the cave system.

"What is this place?" Orion asks, his eyes wandering the concrete walls around us.

"A bomb shelter. Once we realized the dragons only attacked what they could see, we figured it would be the safest place." Jason replies, leading us through a steel doorway. "We think most of the survivors left live in them as well. We have been in contact with quite a few." He says proudly, gesturing toward the control room now before us.

"I met a woman in Florida; she mentioned that most were in shelters," I add on, eyeing the room around us with amazement.

An array of radio equipment is scattered through the room; two rows of desks with screens and phones lay across it. A giant control monitor with several screens is at the farthest point, where all the desks face.

"Impressive." Midnight exclaims, her eyes lost in thought.

"Indeed. We have used it well, scanning for any signs of distress." A warmth fills my heart at his words. Maybe the humans weren't doing so badly after all. He seems rather proud of the work they have done.

"Have you helped many people?" Orion asks him.

"You could say so. Most of it is just checking in on other shelters, making sure no one is too low on supplies." He replies coolly.

"Would you be able to send recordings from a camera?" Midnight asks.

"I suppose we could. What are you suggesting?"

"Well, you have a camera. And we have a symbol of hope. We should put them together." She gestures to me, making my heart sink slightly. *Symbol of hope?* I question, worrying about what she intends to do. "Besides, telling people on a radio without them seeing is entirely different than them seeing proof." She turns toward me, a fire burning in her eyes.

"You have exposed yourself a few times on accident. Now, it's time to do it for real. Let's show the world that you're alive and well. Nothing crazy, just a short video explaining that you are real and we will help." *A video?* I question, feeling rather indifferent about purposely being on screen. Still, openly coming in front of a camera is the fastest way to spread the news. I just hope we will be able to back it up.

After about an hour of stressful filming with Midnight and a small camera crew telling me precisely what to do, we were finally done. Jason displayed the video to the rest of the people in the shelter, hoping to get their opinions on it. I tried my best to hide during this, as I found that I do not like watching myself talk on video. The script I had read was simple: I intend to kill every dragon I can and free the people once more. They had me end by transforming into my cheetah self, flashing my teeth, and holding my wings high. It was an uncomfortable sight, but they seemed to enjoy it. Midnight's main goal was to give the humans hope of being saved, but I doubt how effective it will be.

Once Jason got the approval of the majority and did some edits, they broadcast it to all the radios and televisions they could. He also sent it to all their neighboring bomb shelters, asking them to do the same. It is only a matter of time before it spreads.

Chapter Sixteen

When Cats Fly

"Relax, it will be fine!" I say to Midnight, trying to hide the annoyance in my voice. We were getting ready to head toward another city. The only problem? It is about two hundred miles away. And there is no way I am going to walk.

"No. There is *no* way I am going to do it." She snaps, stepping away from me once more. Orion tightens his grip on my back as I walk toward Midnight. She has got to be the most stubborn person I have ever met.

"You would rather take weeks to walk there? It will only be a couple of hours, Midnight. I promise. It can be even faster if you two get comfortable enough."

She pins her ears back, looking up at the sky in disgust. "I was carried once by a dragon. A memory I am rather not fond of." She snaps. My mind traces back to the battle, seeing Midnight struggle within the minion's grasp as she watched me stab myself. *My bad.* I realize, thinking how helpless she must have felt.

"I am not a minion. It won't hurt. Let's just try, okay?" I softly smile at her. "We need to be fast, right? I want to start doing this sooner rather than later. We can only do so much on foot."

She sits still for a moment, her eyes still on the clouds above. She takes a deep breath, tilting her nose to the sky, her black fur dancing in the wind. Her eyes come down to meet mine as she lets out a sigh. Without a word, she stands and walks toward me, turning herself sideways so that I can grab her.

"You won't regret this!" I say happily, jumping up into the air just above her. Orion lurches backward from the quick change, tightening his grip on me. I extend my claws, firmly grasping them around Midnight's back and under her belly. Her body immediately tenses up, preparing to be lifted into the sky.

"I'll go slow," I say, trying to hide my excitement. It's about time I get to fly with her.

"Let's just get this over with." She replies with shakiness in her voice. I nod my head toward her before thrusting us into the air. Orion adjusts himself on my back, his fingers tightly hooking onto one of my spikes, sending an uncomfortable feeling throughout me.

I close my eyes briefly and take a deep breath to push the feeling out. This is the first time someone has been on my back since Justin, and my heart does not approve. Emily was the only other person to ride me, and I have no idea if she is even alive. *God, I hope she is.* I say to myself, taking another breath.

Trying to distract myself, I focus on Midnight, who is still as stiff as a board inside my claws. I loosen my grip on her slightly as we level out, trying to make her more comfortable. The less I squeeze her with my claws, the better.

"Open your eyes, Midnight. Look!" I say to her, feeling the anxiety course through her body. Only one of us should be miserable, and it shouldn't be her.

"I certainly will not! Cats are *not* supposed to fly." Her voice shakes out. A small laugh escapes me, causing her to tense up even more.

"Okay, well, I am not afraid to admit this is pretty cool." Orion states, his body relaxing slightly as he speaks. I nod in agreement, staring at the clouds around us. It is a beautifully warm day, the air gently tickling my scales as we go.

The ground below us is also an amazing sight; the forests are breaking apart to reveal various towns, each separated by the trees and hills around them. The buildings themselves are small enough to look like building blocks. Being up here makes everything else seem so…small.

Flying is usually my peace when there isn't an anxious cat in my claws and a man on my back that isn't him. What I would give to feel Justin clinging to my back as I dove through the clouds once more. My heart warms at the thought. *We had a lot of good memories.* I think to myself, trying to remember the good parts of him. It isn't hard; there were too many to count.

He was the optimist between us, having more than enough for both of us. My encourager. He told me I could do anything, and I sometimes believed him. Now, I want nothing more than to prove him right. Show him that he did not die in vain, that not killing me wasn't a mistake.

I take a deep breath as I push the thought of him out, not wanting to make our flight more stressful than it already was. I feel for Midnight again, surprised to notice that her body had relaxed.

"Did you fall asleep, Midnight?" Her body shifts slightly at the question.

"No, I just finally opened my eyes…" She answers, her voice full of awe. My lips curl into a smile at the thought. "The world sure is beautiful from up here."

"Well, anytime you want to see it. Just let me know." I reply, feeling glad that she could finally understand it, that we could have yet another thing to talk to each other about.

"Is that Detroit?" Orion asks as a city comes into view. I nod slightly, gently angling us for a decent toward it. A ping of anxiety enters me as we approach. I had become so wrapped up in the flight here that I almost forgot why we were going.

Marcus had told me that the bunker near here is under a lot of stress, as dragons seem to enjoy plaguing the area. There are rumors that Lucifer walks these streets, recruiting anyone he can. These ideas fill all three of us with disgust.

As we get closer to the ground, I eye an empty parking lot that looks big enough to land in. I approach as slowly as possible, preparing myself to hover just above the ground so Midnight can land safely. I have to make sure she will be willing to fly with me again.

"Don't land on me." She squeals as her feet touch the ground. I immediately release my grip on her, watching as she scurries out of the way. I fold my wings in and drop, letting out a sigh of relief. My claws ache slightly; they had never carried something for so long before. I bend my neck toward the ground and lay my wing flat so Orion can jump off. A guilty relief fills me as his touch leaves my back.

"I'm impressed," Midnight starts, a proud look in her eyes. "Your flying skills are excellent." I nod to her before shifting into my human form, happy to be on two normal feet once more. Now it is time for the real work to begin.

Chapter Seventeen

The City

We walk through the middle of the street as a unit, Midnight and Orion at my sides. I am in my human form, spreading my wings to make myself more visible. Our main goal is to be seen, so we are as dramatic as possible. Midnight and I are reaching out to things around us, searching for signs of life. So far, there is nothing. Orion is the most hopeful one of the three of us, keeping our minds at ease and making us relax.

Midnight wanted to ensure we scanned the entire surface before worrying about the people in the shelter, as she dreaded going back underground. I can't blame her, though.

"Marcus said the people here were dealing with many dragons, didn't he? I doubt any survivor wouldn't be underground." I say after an hour of walking.

Midnight shakes her head. "I doubt everyone wants to spend their time hiding underground. We must be sure, so we can try to help them." I stop in my tracks, encouraging them to do the same.

"How can we even help them? We don't have the supplies."

"By giving them hope. They can tell us where the dragons like to linger, and we will wipe them out. That has been the plan all along." She answers confidently, reminding me why we are here in the first person.

"So, we are just using them to seek a fight?" I question, not really sure as to what I expected.

Midnight gives me a nod, a stern expression on her face. "That's exactly what we are going to do. Remember, we are no longer hiding young one. If you want to save the people, you must seek out Lucifer's minions openly. Send them back to the desert with their tails between their legs." I study her for a moment, only finding sincerity and fierceness in her eyes.

I turn my attention to Orion, who is sitting idly by. He straightens himself up some at my gaze. "You barely know how to fight, and you'd have us going after every dragon we see?" He swallows hard.

"If that is what we must do." My heart drops somewhat, thinking of Orion fighting with almost no experience. Although he didn't die in the fight in the meadow, so there's something.

"Alright, then. Let's go find something to kill." I say, my tone flat. I knew better than try and argue with both of them. Part of me knew Midnight was right. It would be tactical to attack as many dragons as we could. It will draw in the attention of any possible allies and hopefully send the minions running home. After all, our main goal is to help the humans.

After another hour of walking, a shiver runs down my spine.

"Stop," I raise my hand at them both, my attention going to the nearby skyscraper. "I think there's a dragon over there," I whisper, pointing toward it.

Midnight steps forward, her eyes locking on it. Her whiskers twitch slightly, and she curls her nose. "I sense it too. Let's go."

Without another word, we all swiftly make our way toward the building. The warning within my blood strengthens, making my hairs stand on end. I shift into a dragon immediately, my eyes moving to Orion as he shifts.

There's more than one. I warn them both, reaching for their minds.

There's something else, too. Midnight replies, crouching herself down behind a smashed car. I fought to roll my eyes; she acted like there wasn't a large dragon standing next to her. It is nearly impossible to hide now.

"Please! Have mercy!" A woman shrieks from within the building, her pounding heart filling my ears. *Human.* I tell myself, instantly straightening myself up. A loud crash answers her cry, the sound of metal and glass breaking.

"If you join us, we will." A cold voice hisses. Orion creeps behind a barrier to my right, trying to get a better view.

'Careful. He's not alone.' I say to him, my eyes flickering to the side of the building, where a pale-yellow dragon carefully crept around. I hold my ground, keeping completely still as another dragon appeared from the other side, their attention on the woman within.

"We will tear this building down if you don't come out." A woman's voice threatens behind her dragon fangs.

The yellow dragon smiles, letting a plume of smoke come out of his nose. "It will be our pleasure either way."

"I'd rather burn alive than submit to you!" She screams. *Ouch.* I think to myself, watching as one of the dragons turns his gaze to the other before his eyes flick to me. I can almost feel his heart drop from within his chest.

"Angel's here!" He shouts, trying to hide the shakiness in his voice. The female dragon instantly turns toward us, hatred in her eyes.

"Lucifer will have our heads if we let her get away." She hisses, an angry trail of smoke fuming from her nose. With her words, a third dragon flies into view, landing hard in front of them. He is slightly larger, his scales a shimmering red. *Three?* I ask myself, a nervous feeling rising in my chest as my eyes go from Midnight to Orion.

Their leader takes a few awkward steps forward on his wings. His eyes locked on mine.

'Focus on the other two. I will help you soon enough.' I reach out to them once more. They stay silent, their gazes on the dragon's facing them.

I lunge forward, teeth blazing as I come at the red one. He jumps to the side, abruptly turning to face me once more. I let out a growl as I lower myself, my eyes locked on his. I reach for him, feeling the anxiety within his body. An image flashed through his mind; the story of how Lucifer's army fell the first time. *You're afraid of me.* I think to myself, allowing my anger to take control as I gaze at him. Darkness swirls inside me, making me let out a menacing growl that makes even Midnight shudder, her attention shifting to me for a split second. *You should be afraid.*

I lunge at the dragon again, anger toward Lucifer building in my body like a fire. I easily tear into his neck, making him shout a muffled shriek as I bite down. As the blood fills my mouth and he breathes his last, a sickening feeling starts to creep through me. I should feel sick, regretting having to kill another life. Yet, I can't help but feel triumphant. *What is wrong with me?* I question, trying to cast out my joy in killing him.

Ignoring the feeling, I shake his body hard and release him. He falls to the ground hard and still. My attention turns to Orion, who is currently on the back of the yellow dragon. He is planted firm, his claws and teeth sunk in while the dragon spins violently underneath him.

He needs to let go. I approach him, ready to slam into the dragon before it takes flight. Before I get close enough, Midnight jumps at its throat and latches on, clawing her way into it.

I turn my head away, feeling queasy at the sight of the bloody mess. The joyful feeling seeped out of me, turning to worry. *How many minions must we kill before Lucifer calls them back to him?* My body shudders at the thought. *They chose this.* I reassure myself. *What kind of person makes a deal with the devil? They deserve this.* I let the thought come into my mind. *They deserve this.* I continue to repeat.

"Are you alright, Angel?" Orion pulls me from my thoughts.

"That growl you did was terrifying." He adds a bit of concern in his voice.

"I'm fine." I lie, trying to keep my tone as calm as possible. "I am just excited to be making a difference."

"She is just rather… dedicated to our cause." Midnight assures him, her voice full of warmth. "On another matter, though," Her voice hardens some. "You must remember that being latched onto a dragon's back is not a place you want to be. I think we need to do some more training." Orion lets out a defeated sigh.

Chapter Eighteen

"Not the back"

Midnight sighs as I toss Orion to the side with my tail, sending him crashing into a nearby fence.

"Sorry." I wince, watching as she shakes himself off. His eyes glow brightly in response as he lowers his body down for another strike. *He's determined; I'll give him that.* I say to myself, watching him closely as he breaks into a run. He comes to my side, jaws wide as he tries to latch onto my wing. I give it a hard flap, sending him rolling backward in a gust of air.

"He makes his intent too clear; I can read what he's about to do before he even tries without looking into his mind," I say to Midnight, making Orion's ears lay flat. I ignore him; I refuse to go easy when his life is at stake. Midnight claimed to have trained with him over the years, but their time was usually short…and there was only so much she could do compared to an actual dragon.

"She's right. You must be more discrete like this." Midnight turns toward me, a mischievous look in her eyes. I tilt my head, eyeing her carefully as she comes at me.

She is on me within a second, darting around my body with her warm paws and sharp claws. "You have to take advantage of the size difference," She shouts to him, biting hard on my side. I let out a disapproving grunt and roll my body, trying to knock her off.

"Always be prepared to bail, should they decide to fly." She continues, jumping hard on my exposed stomach to keep me still. My eyes widen momentarily, realizing how easily she outmaneuvered me. "Be fast and take advantage of their panic as they try to catch you."

I shove Midnight off with my claws, giving her an evil stare as I roll back onto my feet. She smiles, turning her attention back to Orion. *Yeah, I get it. You're the wise one.* I think to myself, feeling slightly discouraged.

"Lucifer's minions won't be as strong or fast as Angel. You are used to fighting with support, like the battle all those years ago. But you are weak. You must remember how small you are compared to them and embrace it. Once you do, they will be easy to take advantage of." Her words send a ping of heartache through me, my mind shifting to the image of Orion first entering the battle with us. I was so relieved to see him there. It is terrifying how quickly circumstances can change.

"Let's keep trying, then." Orion suggests, preparing himself for another spar.

We spend the remainder of the day fighting back and forth. Midnight and Orion take turns attacking me, giving us both advice whenever she feels the need. Part of me thought it wasn't doing much good, as Orion barely improved. He must put in much more work to reach Midnight's level.

I wouldn't mind that; fighting with him is a good distraction. It gives me a purpose other than killing every dragon I see, which is a relief. The ping of joy I got from killing that dragon is not sitting too well. *It was because they were torturing that poor woman.* I remind myself. *That's why you're doing this, for them.*

"Um, excuse me?" A shy voice asks from behind Orion. We turn our attention to her, noticing it is the same woman from before. She has a tray in her hands with various fruits and vegetables. She holds it out to Orion, who stands just a few feet away from her now. "I wanted to thank you for saving me. These are all fresh from the greenhouse."

"Thank you," Orion says, happily taking the tray from her and popping a piece into his mouth. She gives him a shy smile before continuing.

"Are you in need of a place to stay?" She adds, scanning the three of us. "I heard the broadcast from the town up North. We are all thankful for you."

"That's very kind of you, but no. We can't risk attracting too much attention to you." I say gently, hoping she will understand. There was no way Midnight would go for staying underground again. The woman nods slightly before turning away, disappearing behind a building.

Orion props himself down on the ground with the tray in his lap. "Care to join me?" He asks. I instantly make my way to him, relieved to finally have something fresh to eat that isn't an animal. I plop down beside him, snatching a few apple slices.

"It was rather kind of them to do this," I say happily. He nods in agreement. "It is good to know that the broadcast worked," I add, relieved to know all of the uncomfortable filming may have been worth it.

"You two enjoy; I am going to go for a hunt. It won't be long." She states, immediately running off toward the distant trees.

"I forget she can't eat stuff like this." Orion sighs, his gaze still on her as she runs.

"It must be strange for her. But she's used to it," I reply, my mind drifting to the cave that was once her home. Midnight didn't care much about life's joys; her focus never changed. "I don't think she would want to live a normal life even if it was handed to her."

"Did she have a life before she…couldn't change back?" He asks.

"Yes. She told me about it once, very briefly. I think it pains her to talk about it." My mind drifted to that night in the cave shortly after we met. She still had the man's bloody shirt, keeping it close to her. It was the only true "human" possession she had.

"I wonder what she looked like before. I bet she was even scarier." His tone lightens some, trying to imagine how fierce her appearance must have been. I nod in agreement. It was probably a good thing we never saw her human form.

Once she returns, we make ourselves comfortable inside an abandoned furniture store, delighted to feel the comfort of beds again. Midnight curls up on a rug, giving herself the appearance of a black mass. Her eyes shift between Orion and me, giving us a once-over before relaxing.

Always the protector. I think to myself, my eyes lingering on her. *What will she do once this is all over? Maybe she can finally relax.* Then again, I don't even know what I will do if we actually succeed.

Chapter Nineteen

City to City

"You don't belong here anymore," I snap, eyeing the dragon before me. We are standing several yards apart in the street in the middle of Chicago. Midnight and Orion stand behind me, their bodies stained with dragon blood. It had been a rather rough day.

The minion's face flashes with anger as he uses his wings to gesture around him. "Look around. You dare come here, murder my companions, and tell *me* to get you. I will leave, carrying your corpse to Lucifer!" He snaps, lunging forward.

A spark of excitement jolts through me as our bodies collide, fueling me with energy as I rip away at his scales. The feeling has become all too familiar now, as my body seems to enjoy getting minion blood on it.

Toward the end of our entanglement, I end up on top of him, pinning him to the ground as his eyes fill with fear.

"And you call me a demon." He hisses. Annoyed by his remark, I tear his throat open and jump off, leaving him gasping for air. I take a deep breath, trying to push the satisfied feeling down. *I can't find joy in this...I can't.* I tell myself, looking around at the scattered bodies. There had been at least ten here, patrolling the streets, searching for any human they could find. We made sure that ended today. Each one I killed felt easier than the last. *This didn't happen before; what is wrong with me?* I question myself. Something is changing inside of me, and it is terrifying.

Midnight walks up to me slowly, her eyes filled with concern. "Are you alright?"

"Yes, fine. It's just hard to see the world like this. I hate myself for being gone for so long." I sigh. "These demons were people once. If I had been here…" I trail off.

"Stop that. It is not your fault; they chose this fate. Lucifer cannot force people to join him." I nod slightly, trying to justify it.

"Are you both alright? There was more than we thought." I shift the focus to them, not wanting Midnight to pry. I am not sure how she would feel if she knew I was getting enjoyment out of this, even if I wasn't in control.

"Fine, nothing but a few scratches." Orion answers. "Though, I am not sure how much of this blood is actually mine." He adds, shifting into his human form to examine himself. He is doing much better than before. Adrenaline seems to be in his favor now. Though, it does help that we are constantly seeking out fights. He works exceptionally well under stress, getting used to the feeling of it all.

Chicago is the fourth city we have come to on our quest for blood. It is also the most populated, as most of the ones we have encountered only have a few demons lurking. This makes sense; as the human population grows, so does the demon one.

We haven't stayed in the same place for longer than a week, determined to go as far as we can, making many stops along the way. We aren't sure where we are headed, though Midnight suggested an old shapeshifter village somewhere in Wyoming. She has never been there, so she isn't sure exactly where it is, just that it used to exist. She doubts anyone is left from there, but recent events suggest it is worth looking into.

Planning our route around that destination, we started zigzagging to every city we could, avoiding following a pattern that the minions could figure out. Surprising them gives us the edge we need, especially for Orion's sake. It would also be better to reach Wyoming closer to the spring, as the mountains won't be very welcoming in these colder months.

We all go toward the river, happily scraping the blood off in the cool water. Our trio is intimidating enough to humans without being covered in red splatters. It is a good feeling to be clean again, though my body longs for a hot shower.

"Where should we go next?" I ask Midnight as she comes to shore, shaking the wetness from her fur. She stretches in the grass and lets out a yawn before answering.

"Where would you like to go? You spent most of your life locked in the same forest. You're free now. You choose the next place." *Free.* I repeat to myself, my mind instantly thinking of Lucifer. In no way is traveling from city to city without a real home free. I realized long ago that I would never be truly free while he was alive. Even then, what is freedom?

Still, the thought of being able to choose our next target has some appeal to it. *Where would I want to go?* California, maybe. The opposite side of the country from where that battle took place. Although, why should I stop there? Surely Lucifer has minions worldwide, not just in the United States. But that would be too far off our current course.

"How about Nashville?" I suggest saying the first city that popped into my head. "We haven't gone south yet. That's in Tennessee, right?" Midnight tilts her head, thinking for a moment. "It would be warmer."

"Seriously, where do you really want to go?" She asks again. My heart sinks as the first thought pops into my head.

"Home." I let the words slip out. For the first time in months, the memory of Maggie floods my mind again, my adopted mother, whom I had loved more than my own family, apart from Emily. She treated me like her own, despite how different I was. How I longed to see her again. Midnight never told me where she was, if she was even alive. Still, I know there is no way I could see again. My presence alone would endanger her far more than anything else…not that it mattered. I killed her only son.

Midnight's expression hardens, a flicker of guilt flashing through her eyes. She knows exactly what I meant. "Nashville it is, then," I whisper, walking off before she can reply. I refuse to show too much emotion to her now, not with everything at hand. It isn't worth it.

Before long, the sound of Orion's cautious footsteps distracts me. He sits down quietly beside me, a hint of nervousness lingering around him.

"She was like a mother to you, wasn't she? Maggie, right?" He asks gently. I nod my head, keeping my gaze on the water. This was the same man that had found me sleeping on the old battlefield, covered in tears. Surely, I can't make his image of me much worse. "Well, if she was strong enough to raise you, I am sure she is doing just fine." His words warm my chest slightly.

"The girl she raised killed her only son and disappeared while the world around her became chaotic. I must have caused her so much pain." I reply, holding back tears as the image comes to mind. "I wonder if she had a funeral for him, not that I would have been brave enough to go."

"Stop that." He snaps, annoyance in his voice. He gently grabs my face, forcing me to meet his gaze. I let out a soft sob, trying to hold it in. "How many times do I have to tell you it wasn't your fault? He controlled you." I close my eyes and push him away, guilt rising in my chest.

"Yes, he did control me. But I fell into the trap. I so foolishly thought he would meet me in open combat again. He knows what I was created for. The devil is supposed to be clever, right? I should have noticed the signs."

Orion stays silent for a moment. His eyes focused intently on the river as he thought about his reply.

"You were young, caught up in the idea of winning. You saw him there; that man had been ruining your life, trying to get you and your loved ones killed—the one who would kill innocents, luring them into his cause and keeping their souls for himself. Anyone with a right mind would have done the same. You saw a chance to end him and took it."

The weight of his words on me is shocking. I know he is right; I wanted to. I tried to kill him, to do what I was created for. But it was too rash.

"We should have known that the four of us couldn't have possibly won," I say, the words like a dagger in my heart. *Did Midnight think we would win?* She is the most intelligent person I know. She believed we had a chance; that must count for something.

"But that was the past. Bring yourself to the here and now. We are doing this right. Picking away at his army and hopefully gaining a following. We will make this right, even if we have to kill a thousand minions one by one." *Why is he so good with words?* I ask myself, already feeling the hope rise in my chest.

We weren't meant to win then. There was no way we could. But now we have a real chance. And it doesn't matter how many dragons I must kill to accomplish it.

"Okay. Let's go kill some dragons." I conclude, standing up on my feet once more. *I just hope this darkness inside me stays in control.* The thought of this happy feeling getting stronger with each kill…how many is too many before I am no longer myself?

Chapter Twenty

Nashville

We made it to Nashville by the next afternoon, a new sense of determination coursing through me. Orion's talk with me was a good reminder of why we are doing this. The increase in heat is also nice, as the winter air from the north was starting to creep in, which is unpleasant when you're sleeping in the woods.

The city would have been breathtaking had it not been covered in rubble and collapsing buildings. A large river flows through the city, littered with debris from the fallen bridges, and only God knows what else. Cars are littered everywhere, most with their doors still wide open. *This place must have been hit hard.* I think to myself as we approach.

"I'm going to kill Lucifer. Just look at what he has done." I snap as we descend, the smell of smoke and blood filling my nose. Orion tightens his grip on me, a mix of anger and fear coursing through him. Part of me is glad he is angry; it will be easier for him to fight. I scan the area for a place to land, noticing a relatively clear parking lot near the river.

"I'm sure there are survivors. This city is huge; hopefully, they also have a shelter." Orion tries to hide the uneasiness in his voice.

"He's building an army by spreading fear," I reply, gently setting Midnight down before we land. She immediately shakes her body, followed by a big stretch.

"I hate flying." She hisses, seeming to ignore mine and Orion's conversation. She looks around momentarily, watching silently as I shift into my human form. Although I enjoy flying much more than her, it is nice to be back on two feet, especially when carrying extra cargo.

I go to the river, momentarily stopping to admire the trees planted on the banks. "At least some of the trees are still alive," I say, gently rubbing one of its leaves between my fingers as I take a deep breath. Longingness sweeps through me, remembering how Justin and I would run through the forest together, finding happiness despite our impending doom; what I would give to feel like that again.

Now I'm here, in a completely different state. Nothing but a broken world and relentless dragons, spreading chaos as they go. I will do anything to give the people back some peace.

"Let's rest for a while. Then we can rid this place of the minions." I suggest making myself comfortable in the grass. Midnight joins me, followed by Orion.

"Should we be resting out in the open like this?" Orion asks, looking nervously at the river in front of us.

"It's perfect. They'll find us before we find them." I smile, spreading my wings out around me. *Just let me have this moment.* I think to myself, enjoying the feel of the grass under my feathers.

Orion tries to protest but is quieted by Midnight, who is happily soaking in the sun. I am not the only one disliking all this traveling.

We spend the rest of the afternoon lying there, sprawled out in the fading sun, ignoring the deadly smell of the river we were by. There was no telling how many corpses were hiding in there. *God, have mercy on them. They've suffered so much already.*

As I fade into darkness, I drift off into a dream.

I'm standing in a large space, surrounded by darkness. A voice whispers in my head.

"Kill. I need more. Kill…kill…kill…" It repeats.

"I will kill any minion I see," I reply, trying to see into the void, but there's no one there.

"Kill…kill them all…"

"Who are you?" I ask, desperately searching in the darkness.

"I am you. Now, kill. Kill the demons and feed me. We must become stronger."

"You are not me." I snap, anger rising within me. "Are you what is making me…enjoy killing?" I shudder at the question. I wait for a response, to no avail. "Leave me! I don't know how I can't feel you but leave! You don't belong here." I start to run through the darkness, searching for anything to help.

Nothing is here. 'Where am I?' I ask myself.

"Wake up. Trouble is near." The voice warns suddenly, sending a shiver through me. "Wake!"

My eyes snap open, and I spring to my feet, nearly falling over from the fast movement. *What just happened?* I ask myself. I look toward Midnight, whose gaze on me freezes instantly, her eyes widening. If she didn't have fur, you could see the color drain from her face.

"What?" I question, panic rising in my chest. She closes her eyes for a moment and shakes her head, followed by a quick release of air.

"Your wings…and your eyes. They were…" She trails off, staring at me in disbelief. I turn to look at them, only seeing their normal colors. *What is she going on about?* I question. She looked at me like I was a ghost…

"They were black," Orion speaks up from behind me. "You woke us up with your mumbling." My eyes were black? And my wings? Surely, that was just a dream. There is no way that was real.

"I was having a nightmare. That's all." I stammer, trying to ignore the fear coursing through me.

"You're changing, Angel. You may not feel it, but that darkness in you is growing. It must be a side effect of being possessed by Lucifer." *That's right. That's what it is. That dream was just that.* I comfort myself, feeling more okay with Midnight's conclusion than mine.

"Makes sense to me," I reply coolly, prompting Midnight to tilt her head slightly.

"You're okay with that?"

"I mean, it's better than what I was thinking. Makes much more sense too. Plus, I'm okay. If I must deal with some black wings, so be it. I've dealt with worse. I'm still me." I speak fast, trying to keep my composure. Midnight isn't convinced.

"What's your theory?" She asks, her green eyes staring intently into mine. *That the dream I had before I woke up wasn't a dream.*

"It's silly, and I highly doubt it's true," I say, trying to push it off. She rolls her eyes and starts speaking, but not before Orion cuts her off again.

"Do you feel that?" He asks, looking up toward the dark sky. *Oh, good. Dragons.* I think, feeling almost happy about their arrival. They chose the perfect time to make themselves known.

We immediately spread ourselves out, preparing for the trio of dragons flying above us. I shift into a dragon, letting a rush of determination fill me. We have a purpose, including allowing Lucifer to know his minions aren't welcome anymore.

The three of them go into a dive, seeming to be focused on Orion, who has yet to shift. *Come on, now.* I think to myself, feeling slightly annoyed with his idleness.

I leap from the ground and position myself above him, flying straight at the others. In a panic, two of the three move to the side as I collide with the middle one. A ping of pain comes through me as their claws grasp my scales, digging into me to hang on.

We fall toward the ground, entangled together as we bite at each other's throats. This one has a strong will, but they are outmatched. With one swift move, I reach for their neck, snapping it with my jaws.

By the time I land on the ground, their body falls a few feet from me. Satisfied, I turn toward Orion, who is scurrying on top of one of them. Midnight is already rushing to help, leaving her victim to bleed out in the river.

'They must be killed.' The voice from my dream whispers in my mind, filling me with anger.

'They will be. She ripped his throat open.' I reply, trying to close my mind off from whatever was there, feeling nothing. *How can I not feel you?* I shudder, turning my attention toward Orion once more.

Midnight is already on top of the now belly-up dragon, slicing one of its wings as Orion bites into its throat. *That seems a bit much.* I think to myself, watching the two of them with open shock.

"Surely there are more. Let's find them." I say once they finish, hoping to rid myself of the strange feeling lingering inside.

By the time the sun sets again, we had encountered twelve minions. All of which were now sent back to Lucifer. The dark feeling inside me grew with each kill, as I was responsible for eight deaths.

Every kill had added just a sliver of growth to the dark feeling, making me anxious about how much more killing we had yet to do. Yet I know that can't stop me, as saving everyone is far more important than my own well-being, even if I must embrace this darkness to do it.

Chapter Twenty-One

Lucifer

Lucifer paced the room, anger rising within his chest. Another bunch of his demons had just been killed; he could feel it. One after the other, his connections are severing. Their souls are being sent back to Hell, where they are useless to him…for this, at least.

He had freely allowed them to venture the Earth, doing as they pleased and killing as many humans as possible. They were supposed to spread fear, so his army could continue growing. He had given several of them the power to make deals through him, taking anyone that begged for mercy. He needs all of the help he can get.

Not that any of that mattered now. They were dying and fast. It had been nearly a year since Angel escaped his grasp, and here he stood, with almost three hundred of his army gone. Not killing her was one of the biggest mistakes he ever made. That much was clear to him now.

Why had he been so naïve to try and keep her? He was supposed to be the clever one. *You let the idea of power get to your head.* He reminded himself, clenching his fists in anger. He turns toward his right hand, their eyes meeting. Despite how much he hated it, Lucifer knew what he had to do now.

"Leo, it's time. I can't handle any more—" He staggers for a moment, another blow of deaths suddenly coming to him. He lets out a gasp and steadies himself. "She's in LA." He takes a deep breath before shaking his head. "We have so many there."

"What is it we need to do?" Leo asks, staring intently at him. He is one of the few people Lucifer trusts and the only man he knows that wouldn't run at the tiniest hint of freedom.

"Call them back." He answers, closing his eyes and reaching for all of those he has left. It only takes him a few seconds to feel them all at their various locations worldwide. Most are already here with him, hiding safely in the desert.

'Come.' He says firmly, reaching all their minds at once. He doubted that Angel would be dumb enough to come for him here, knowing how it went the last time they fought. He is sure that he will be able to attack her mind again. Still, her growing power wouldn't be worth the risk.

Lucifer makes his way to his makeshift throne room in the heart of his warehouse. It wasn't much, but it would do just fine for now. By the time he climbs onto this black throne, about thirty of his men are standing around in the chamber, their anxious eyes on him. Leo stands proudly at his side.

"When the rest get here, I will descend back into Hell. Angel is becoming too big a threat for me to be out in the open, especially since she knows our location. We will do as we were before the first battle, hiding in the shadows."

A few murmurs escape the crowd, along with disapproving glances. *Men and their stubbornness.* He thinks to himself, anger rising in his chest.

"Silence!" Lucifer rises to his feet, prompting the men to bow their heads in submission. "You will do well to listen," He snaps, spreading his wings wide as he towers over them. "We must be patient once more. Hide; let the humans start coming out again. Quietly find lost souls and make them join our cause. I will send you to different locations, where you will stay in your human forms and draw no attention to yourselves. You will be my eyes." He commands, looking over the lot of them carefully.

The men before him are his best soldiers and have all proven to be good at bringing new souls to him. He hopes they will do him good; he needs every soul they can get.

"We have had to do this before. Now, with your help, we will rebuild our army much faster. We can't afford for Angel to continue killing us off." He descends the ten steps to his throne toward the crowd. "Angel is likely giving them hope, slaughtering everyone she sees. She is becoming rather vicious; we must realize you are no match for her now."

He walks through them now, taking slow, long steps as he weaves. "Let's let them expand on their hope for a while." He stops in the middle, pausing momentarily to let his words reach them. "And when it reaches its peak, we will crush them again."

Chapter Twenty-Two

Wyoming

Wyoming is a beautiful state, the thirtieth we have visited so far. It is covered in mountains, with miles and miles of thick, lush forests. If there were shapeshifters here, it would be the perfect hiding place. The journey has been exhausting, draining me of the hope that the other community was still alive. If they are, they are extremely well hidden within these vast mountains.

We have been here two weeks and have not found any evidence of their existence, though Midnight blames me for that. She says the dark feeling I have is likely scaring off anyone within a fifty-mile radius. I do not doubt this, as I can only imagine how much stronger the feeling is now with how many minions we have killed.

"Why don't we split up for a while, then?" I had asked her several times. Her answer is always the same: she wanted to keep an eye on me. She and Orion are growing increasingly worried about me, afraid that this darkness will overcome me eventually. Despite the alarming growth within me, I kept assuring them that I was fine.

I still cannot bring myself to tell her what conclusion I am starting to accept, as it would only lead to more unanswered questions. There is no plausible explanation for how I was in another world, especially while asleep.

That is why I have decided to leave them tonight, at least for a while. Then they might have hope of being approached by another shifter once they feel that the 'threat' is gone. Shapeshifters are very good at feeling each other's presence, but I know I am undoubtedly hindering that.

They will be relatively safe without me, as the dragons have gone extinct. Well, they have gone into hiding, at least. We concluded that Lucifer must have finally called them back, realizing they were no match scattered all about. The tides are finally changing. At least, we hope so. I have lost count of how many dragons I have killed, though I am pretty sure the darkness inside me knows. It has enjoyed every taste of blood I have given to it, so not seeing dragons for three weeks now has been nice.

"We all set for the night?" I ask Orion, who happily makes himself a s'more over our small fire.

"Yep! I still can't believe there was chocolate in that store still."

"And I can't believe you're actually eating it," I reply, remembering how ransacked that store had been. Who knows how long that bar was sitting on the floor?

"It was still in the wrapper; it's fine." He assures me, popping it into his mouth.

"If you say so."

"Will you two hush up and get some sleep?" Midnight groans from beside the fire. "We have a lot more walking to do tomorrow."

"Alright, fine," Orion replies, making himself comfortable. I lay down as well, waiting patiently for them to fall asleep.

Once I know they are, I quietly get up and fasten the sword to my hips. *I'll be back.* I say to myself, watching the two of them sleep peacefully. *Please forgive me.*

'Let's find something to kill.' The voice speaks, making me shake my head in disapproval. I have gotten used to ignoring it, as it usually goes away with time.

I walk several paces away from them before shifting into my cheetah form and taking flight. I have no idea where I am going; just that I need to put some distance between us. They might be angry initially, but it will subside once they find what we seek. *If they find one.* I let the thought come to my head.

I fly higher, letting the cold air take me from my thoughts, leading me through the dark sky. It was a guilty pleasure, enjoying the wind on my wings without the presence of Midnight or Orion. It feels like it has been a lifetime since I have gotten to fly alone.

I soar through the sky until it becomes day, the sun rising to create a beautiful orange and red glow in the clouds. I take a deep breath, enjoying the smell of the open air. *There is nothing better than being up here.*

I hold onto my glimpse of happiness, rolling and diving within the sunrise, my chest glowing with a warmth I hadn't felt in a long time. I hope I'll be free someday. Why I had to be chosen for this seemingly impossible task, I couldn't answer. But it sure is fun to enjoy the little freedom I have.

With the rising sun, I close my mind to ensure that Midnight can't reach me. It would take her days to get here anyways. I was out of the mountains, flying above grass fields and scattered farms.

Everything below me looked surprisingly intact, a lucky town hidden deep in the country. The minions did not care to go where the people weren't. A crossroads comes into view, with a few buildings sitting around it. All of which were still in good shape. Intrigued, I descend toward them. There could be people there from the looks of things, and that was a chance I was willing to take.

As I approach the intersection, a faint rustling sound fills my ears, prompting me to look toward a small cornfield. Nothing moves. *Probably just an animal.* I conclude, turning my attention back to the landing zone.

I landed in the middle of the intersection, in front of a building that was the most eye-catching of all. *A church.* Something I had never stepped foot in my entire life, too afraid of what might happen. *Would I even be worthy of stepping inside?* He supposedly created me to do a task that I have miserably failed at, resulting in thousands of deaths. *No way.*

I take a few steps back, staring at the building with turmoil. The white doors and large, unbroken windows looked incredibly inviting. *It's just a building,* I say to myself, starting to walk forward. *I should see if anyone is in there.* I shift into my human form, thinking it's best not to parade around as a cheetah with wings. Not that a human with wings is much better.

I softly opened the doors, peering inside with wide eyes. *No one.* Relieved, I make my way down the aisle. Several rows of pews are on either side, all facing a center stage slightly elevated above them. In the center is a pedestal with a small microphone attached.

"Just a building," I repeat, gently running a finger over one of the wooden pews. I hold it over my face, expecting to see a layer of dust. *Nothing.* It is spotless. *Someone has been cleaning this.* I realize, looking around at the well-kept building. Books and notes sit in storage boxes in the pews, with a few blankets here and there. *There are people here.* I think excitedly.

I go to one of the pews, sitting down to inspect one of the books. My hair suddenly stands on end as the door creaks from behind me.

I snap around, freezing at the sight of a man standing in it, his curious eyes on me. "I was curious to see which one of those dragons was brave enough to enter the church. It seems it wasn't a dragon at all." I lay the book down and rise to my feet, making the man take a few steps back.

"No, I am not. I'm—"

"I know who you are! The question is, why is our supposed savior giving off such dark energy?" He cuts me off; his voice is full of distrust.

I lower my hands, letting my wings droop slightly as well. "I assure you, I mean you no harm. I saw the town untouched and…" *Wait. He can feel my dark energy.* "you're a shapeshifter, aren't you?" I changed the subject, realization setting in.

"Yes, and I will do anything to protect the good people here." He says, an edge building in his voice.

"As will I. Surely you have heard the news about me. I have been traveling the country, killing all the dragons I encounter. You're no minion. I can feel the good in you." I say to him, trying to ease the tension.

He stays silent for a moment, looking me over carefully. "Show me, then. It is said that the chosen one's true form is a cheetah with wings. Then I might believe you." He decides, nodding his head slightly. *Show him. Why can't they just believe me?*

I sighed before moving myself from the row to make more room. His eyes instantly go to the sword strapped to my waist, a flicker of hope going through them. As I shift, the tension in the room lifts.

I spread my wings out wide to show they are still there. "Believe me now?" His lips curl into a smile, and he nods slightly before shifting into a giant beast. My eyes widen as I examine him. He was a cat, no doubt about it, but he also had wings. And a large beak where his mouth should be. His front legs had feathers extending into large talons. The back of his body was entirely fur, with giant cat-like feet—*a griffin.* I conclude, thinking back to the Sanctuary.

"I trust you, Angel. Especially with that sword attached to you. Would you care to go fly with me?" He turns toward the exit, gesturing toward the sky.

Without another word, he takes off into a run with his brown wings spread wide. I follow suit, leaping into the air behind him. He gracefully ascends into the sky, moving at a surprising pace.

'Where are you taking me?' I reach out to his mind, instantly feeling his connection.

'To my family. They'll be happy to see you.' A warm glow fills me with hope. I had left Midnight in hopes of her finding more shapeshifters, and it had been the other way around. There was no way she could stay mad at me now.

He leads me toward the mountains, the same ones I had just come from. *We were closer than we thought.* I scowl, realizing it was my fault that we couldn't find them, despite being so close.

'When we get there, let me do the talking, alright? You might scare them off. We have felt your presence for a couple of weeks, so it might be alarming for them.' He warns me, making his descent toward the cliffs.

We land on a flat rock just outside a small cave entrance. *Shifters and their caves.* I think to myself.

"Stay here; I'll only be a minute." He says, shifting into his human form before slipping through the entrance. I focus on the cliff's edge, the breath leaving my lungs instantly.

We are sitting far above a forest, nestled safely in the middle of the mountains. A large lake sits in the middle of a valley, with a winding river extending through the trees. *I could disappear in there.* The thought invades my mind, longing for the forest I used to call home. *He might make going back possible.*

I close my eyes and take a deep breath. I can't waste my time wishing for that anymore. A tear slides down my fur, making me shake my head. *No.* I push the feelings away, turning back toward the cave entrance. I have bigger things to worry about. I am on a cliff outside of a griffin's home.

"What if she—" A young woman's voice protests from within the cave, being cut off as she gets shoved into the light. I perk myself up, tilting my head slightly at the sight of her being pulled by the man. Behind them both is an older woman whose eyes instantly meet mine. The soft green undertones give me some comfort. She has shapeshifter blood in her.

The younger girl freezes once she notices me, her face turning white. I curl my lips into a gentle smile and bring my wings close to my sides, trying to look smaller.

"Laviana, Phaenna, meet Angel. She is here to help us." He says proudly, nodding in my direction.

The younger girl, Laviana, stands up a little straighter, the color slowly returning to her face. Her bright green eyes sparkle in the sun, soft brown hues dancing in them. She clears her throat, keeping her gaze on my feet. "Hello, Angel. I am Boreas's daughter." Her voice comes out soft and quiet.

I nod my head slightly, trying to ease her anxiety. "Pleased to meet you," I reply with the gentlest tone I can muster. She smiles and bows her head.

"We want to make you an offer," Boreas explains. "We have been hiding from the world for quite some time, about thirty years, to be exact. As we felt the other shapeshifters…disappearing, we no longer felt safe in the open. Now that we can feel that the dragons are finally going away, we want to help." He pauses, trying to read my expression.

"What do you have in mind?"

"Well, we wish to join your side. I've been scouting the surrounding areas to see how things are going. I have heard many rumors about you, going around slaughtering the dragons Lucifer has sent." A spark lights in my chest.

"We are sick of hiding. We are all that's left of our tribe, my family and me. All we ask is that you protect us. Let us come with you wherever it is you're going." *Where am I going?* I ask myself.

We had been traveling the country trying to rid it of Lucifer's minions, yet we had no real destination. Although, the Sanctuary in Michigan could be an answer for them. Surely by now, Arkadia's people will have learned about our success. *But will she accept us back?* I couldn't even answer that. She is Midnight's oldest friend, so there could be a chance. It sounds a lot better than traveling around the countryside any longer.

"Angel?" Boreas pulls me from my thoughts; his eyes are full of longing. His daughter and who I could assume was his wife, was standing idly by his side.

"I will do my best. I can take you to Midnight, my mentor. We were recently at a sanctuary in the Dark Pines Forest. It likely has the last remaining shapeshifters in it. I can get you there, but I am not sure I will be allowed in myself."

"There are more out there!" Laviana exclaims excitedly, hope filling her eyes.

"Many," I say, meeting her gaze with a warm smile. "A saw a child shift into a griffin, like your father." Laviana's expression brightens even more.

"Then what are we waiting for? Let us go." Phaenna speaks, pushing herself from her husband and transforming into a dazzling silver griffin. *This is what it's about.* I think to myself, reaching out to Midnight for the first time in hours. It is finally time to show Arkadia there's hope out there.

Chapter Twenty-Three

Back Again

We find Midnight and Orion waiting by the lakeshore, chatting quietly while looking at the water. I land first, gesturing for the family to wait while I make my presence known, not that they can't feel me from afar.

Midnight swiftly turns around at the sound of my purposely heavy footsteps, her eyes instantly going into a glare. "About time! How dare you run off without telling us!" She scowls, flattening her ears at me.

"I felt you would have more luck finding something. Besides, I do not come alone." I reply, gesturing toward the woods behind me. They both tense up, their eyes cautiously watching the tree line. "You can come out now," I call out to them.

Boreas comes first, followed by Laviana and Phaenna, still in their griffin forms. He dips his head slightly in the form of a greeting, his eyes on Midnight. Laviana keeps her head low, her now golden eyes soft and gentle. She is the smallest of the three, keeping her wings tight to her sides to make herself appear even smaller. I can't help but feel protective over her, wanting nothing more than for her to come out of her shell.

Midnight's expression changes at the sight of them, hope and excitement filling her eyes. She quickly steps toward them, offering a soft smile. Orion walks slightly behind her, his face full of wonder.

"Midnight, Orion, this is Boreas and his family. He approached me while I was exploring a town." I introduce them.

"Pleased to meet you all. I must say, I am surprised to see you. I did not know there were any mountain shifters left. We were beginning to lose hope." Midnight says excitedly.

Boreas's gaze meets mine, gently tilting his head toward them. *Straight to the point, huh?* I think to myself. Although, I could only imagine how long they had been hiding up there.

"They wish to join us on our journey. I offered to take them to the Sanctuary." I say coolly. "In exchange, they will join our fight against Lucifer." Midnight's ears instantly perk up, her gaze hardening some.

"I see." She says quietly, seeming to contemplate the statement.

"Arkadia might not welcome me back, but surely she cannot deny three new faces."

"I think she will welcome you back," Orion speaks up. I turn my attention to him, tilting my head slightly. "Well, remember how you left it? From what you two told me, I'm sure it is in turmoil now. Especially with the disappearance of the dragons."

That sounded appealing enough. "So, what do you say, Midnight? Let's take them to her. It might even put us in good favor. Besides, isn't this what we have wanted all along? To bring new shapeshifters to her, to prove there is hope?" I try and convince her. I doubted Arkadia would allow us back if Midnight weren't by our side.

Midnight thinks for a moment, staring toward the lake once more. She had known Arkadia long ago and knew her best.

"Yes, let's take them." She finally answers, her gaze meeting Boreas's daughter. "Just know that this will be dangerous, flying across the country, especially if you decide to help us fight Lucifer. We can't promise your lives." She adds more seriousness to her tone.

"I have spent my entire life hiding," Laviana says quietly. "Let us go before it is too late." Her father gives her a look of sympathy before giving his wings a big stretch in response.

I nod in agreement, moving away from the group to shift into my dragon form. "I don't want to alarm you, so be prepared," I warn them, turning into the giant beast. Boreas's eyes widen slightly, but he holds his ground. Orion swiftly climbs onto my back, hoping to ease their fear.

Without a word, I jump into the air and snatch Midnight with my claws. The three of them follow suit, joining me in the air once more.

"Is this how you have been traveling?" Boreas questions, staring at me with amusement.

"Yes. It is not ideal, but it works. Now, we have a long way to go. Best not to delay." I reply, angling myself toward the clouds as I lead them East.

By the time we reached Michigan, four hours had passed. We learned several things about the Griffin family. For one, Boreas is nearly ninety years old but looks like he is in his thirties. He claims that all shapeshifters are this way. Our fast-healing abilities make for longer lives.

We also learn that when his tribe started getting taken out by Lucifer's minions, he took his family into hiding to keep them safe. The sanctuary that was in Wyoming was found by Lucifer and suffered an attack from nearly fifty dragons. With only about ten of them remaining, they never stood a chance. He had managed to get his wife and newborn daughter out in time, but it was too late for the others. They will never forget that day and have always wanted revenge.

We touch down about two miles from the Sanctuary itself, as it is impossible to enter it from the sky if you don't know where to look.

"It's so thick here! No wonder Lucifer hasn't found this one." Boreas exclaims, shaking a few twigs out of his wings. We had a relatively tight landing.

"Yes, it is probably best to travel the rest of the way in human forms. But it is getting rather late. Arkadia might think we are attacking if we try to get in at night. Best we wait until morning." Midnight commands, making herself comfortable on a pile of leaves.

"Do you think they can feel my presence? Camping out here might scare them." I question. Midnight shakes her head.

"Unlikely, we did not notice you until you were outside the barrier. One of the downfalls of the magic."

"I don't know if I can sleep; it is much warmer here." Pheanna pipes up, stretching out on a bed of moss. "Sure is nice to be deep in the forest, though."

I nod in agreement. After nearly a year of traveling to various locations, I am finally back in my forest. The same forest I grew up in, welcoming me with its dark woods, concealing everything deep inside. I close my eyes, letting the sounds of the birds soothe me to sleep. *It feels good to be home.* I smile, letting my mind drift away.

When the morning comes, we do not hesitate to approach the entrance. Midnight leads the way, effortlessly maneuvering through the thick brush as we struggle behind her in our human forms. I do my best to keep my wings close as they snag every little thing they can.

It isn't long before the familiar row of touching trees comes into view, making their fake wall. Boreas and Phaenna stare with amazement, aware that it is the barrier.

"Can you feel it?" He says excitedly to her, staring in awe. She nods her head, pulling their daughter into an embrace. It sure was nice to see them enjoy a moment of peace. *Arkadia, you better let us in.* I think to myself. There is no way I am going to disappoint this family. *Just let me do some good.*

Midnight steps before us, walking close to the barrier's entrance. She stands completely still, her eyes closed. *She must be reaching out to her.* I conclude, noticing her concentration. Surely Arkadia can feel my presence now.

We all sit patiently behind Midnight, aware of how vital her conversation must be. No one dares to speak, sitting in complete silence.

After several minutes, Midnight turns back to look at us. I hold my breath for a moment, trying to read her expression. *This would be so much easier if you were human.* I try to reach for her mind, only to find she has me closed off. I am met with a disapproving glare before she shifts her focus toward the group.

"Come." She commands, turning back toward the barrier. "Walk straight through, do not hesitate." I breathe a sigh of relief, stepping out of the way so Boreas and his family can go ahead of me.

They all take deep breaths before walking forward, a mixture of excitement and anxiousness coming off them.

They trail Midnight, releasing soft gasps as she walks straight through, disappearing before their eyes. Boreas walks slightly in front of his girls, taking their hands as they touch the barrier. With a soft hum, they disappear as well. *They made it.* I breathe a sigh of relief.

"Go ahead; I'll be right after you," I say to Orion, standing idly beside me. He doesn't move, eyeing me carefully. *No, you can't be a healer right now.* I hope he isn't catching on to the nervousness building inside me.

His presence creeps into my mind, filled with worry. *'What is it?'* He asks, letting his calmness connect to me. *'I can feel the anxiousness in you.'* *Of course, you can.* I try not to groan, not wanting to hear a pep talk right now.

'People with wicked hearts can't enter. What if I can't go in?' I let the truth come, staring intently at the trees in front of us.

'You may have darkness, but you are still pure, Angel. That's nonsense. Come.' He abruptly grabs my hand, pulling me toward the barrier. I heed his pull, slowly following behind him. He stops directly in front, gently squeezing my hand that comforts my body.

Fueled by his encouragement, I take a deep breath. *'Together, then.'* I reply, stepping into the now shimmering barrier.

Chapter Twenty-Four

Emily

Emily enjoyed being in the woods, away from the crowds where the dragons tended to be. They did not care for the forests like they did the cities, which made her feel incredibly lucky that she grew up knowing how to survive.

The day the devil himself came was a true nightmare. She knew it would happen eventually; her sister was proof of that. Still, nothing prepared her for the chaos that followed. She decided to leave Michigan and took her little brother to Wyoming, far from any large cities. She had always wanted to come here to see the mountains. There were none in Michigan, so coming here was amazing, despite the circumstances.

The grief of her sister's death hit her much harder than her brother. She would have treated it much differently if she knew that the birthday would be the last time she saw her. Still, knowing she got to fly with her at least once comforted her. It was one of the most exciting experiences of her life.

She and Jake managed to come upon a small town that seemed untouched by the devil's minions. The townsfolk happily welcomed them, glad to see some new faces. Over time, she began to see them as family. They took her and her brother in, healing and keeping them alive in the ever-changing world.

They had no service out there, as their only cell tower had been destroyed before Emily arrived. Not that this mattered; the news was always the same: "Dragons destroy city." She couldn't care less to hear any more of it. It is too much to bear.

The town had a small church building where they met, giving thanks to God they were all still alive and praying that he would someday stop the madness outside. She had never really been faithful until she learned how real the devil was. If he was around, surely there was a God, too. Then again, she couldn't understand why he would allow such destruction… or why he would let Angel die when they needed her most.

Emily spends most of her time at the church, cleaning it and caring for everything inside. She felt it was her way of giving back to the townsfolk for letting them stay here.

She also found out that her sister was indeed not alone, as she could swear that she saw a cat-like bird flying through the skies occasionally. This made her cling to the hope that more people like Angel were preparing to fight back. *Would it be enough?* She questioned. She had never seen a demon with her own eyes, but if they were like Angel.

She once thought her sister was the most powerful thing, yet the devil himself slew her. Although, how could she stand up against a divine being? She was so young when she died…

The guilt of not finding a way to trap her sister into not fighting lingered inside Emily, filling her with grief. This played a big part in keeping her close to the church, hoping God could forgive her one day. She was the big sister, the protector. Yet, she let her sister get slaughtered. It only got worse from there, as the news enjoyed broadcasting about the death of an angel.

On weekdays, Emily also spent her time in the garden, tending to it and keeping the crops in good shape. It was a great distraction while her brother hunted with the other men.

There, she saw something that filled her with hope once more.

As Emily was fetching some tools to pull weeds, a dark shadow swept over her, filling her with fear. She immediately ran into the corn, praying that she wasn't seen. She takes a few deep breaths, realizing she is safe for now.

Pulled by her curiosity, she slowly crept through the crops, reaching the edge facing the church. New panic swept over her as she watched one of the doors slowly close. *Please don't hurt the church.* She begged. It was one of the few things still keeping her going.

After a few moments, a tremendous swooshing sound filled her ears, causing her to fall backward with a gasp. *I am not crazy!* She thinks to herself, staring in awe at the animal now before her. A large, lion-like beast with wings stood outside the church, eyeing it carefully.

It tilts its head slightly, seeming to be curious about whatever is inside. She holds her breath as it shrinks before her eyes, turning into a man. *A shapeshifter!* She thinks happily, watching as he cautiously opens the church door.

He stands still in the doorway as though he is conversing with whatever is inside. She tries her best to listen, but she is too far, and there is no way she would risk getting any closer.

After a few moments, the man takes a few steps back, letting Emily get a better view of what was inside her church. The breath leaves her lungs as she watches a cheetah walk out of the church with white wings with black tips attached to its back.

Her heart leaps as she notices the eyes; even from here, she can see the beautiful green glow. She looked different, but Emily knew her when she saw those eyes. *Angel.* She stays completely still, her heart pounding in her chest. Her sister is alive, changed, but alive.

The man suddenly transforms back into a cat, gesturing toward the sky with his head. In an instant, both of them are in the air. Emily scurries herself through the crops, running to get a better view.

Tears swell in her eyes as she watches them fly toward the mountains, disappearing into the clouds.

"I will see you again." She whispers, ignoring her brother's calls as he searches for her.

Chapter Twenty-Five

Change

I breathe a sigh of relief as I make it through the barrier safely to the other side. *Maybe it's broken.* I wonder, knowing that the darkness within me is much stronger than before. I give Orion a soft smile before letting go of his hand, feeling thankful for his support. He had truly been a good help to me all this time, believing in me even when I couldn't. *I need him now more than ever.* I think, realizing just how important this next step is.

I turn my attention toward the scene before us. Arkadia is standing in front of the people, their wide eyes on us. She is keeping her posture high, her fierce eyes on me. Midnight gives her a gentle nod, a relieved expression on her face. *Was she afraid I wouldn't make it through?* I question the thought like poison in my head.

"Welcome back, Angel." She says too warmly, a smile playing on her lips. She turns her gaze toward Boreas, who is staring at the crowd behind her with genuine excitement. "And welcome, Boreas, Laviana, and Phaenna. Midnight has informed me that you were lucky enough to bump into Angel."

Boreas clasps his hands together, nodding in agreement. "We are very pleased to be welcomed here; we have been hiding far too long." He answers, the excitement lingering in his voice.

"Midnight also informs me that you intend to join Angel on her seemingly impossible quest, do you not?" She replies, the warmth in her voice fading. *There she is.*

Boreas holds his ground, scanning the people behind her once more. Most faces are on him: men, women, and children. A love fills his eyes, his excitement radiating off of him. It is so clear that he has missed seeing his own kind.

"I do. There will be no more hiding from me." He says confidently, meeting her gaze with a fire of his own. "She has filled us with hope." Arkadia stays still for a moment before turning her gaze back toward me.

"Angel, I do have to apologize to you," She starts. *Did we come all this far to be turned away?* "I underestimated you." *What?* I think, doing my best to keep a neutral expression that turns into a harsh swallow. "It has been weeks since we have felt the presence of a minion, and here you are, standing before me with a small band of shapeshifters at your side." She tilts her head toward Boreas.

"I only want the best for my people, and they have spoken. Now, I do not agree with this in the slightest, but" she pauses, turning toward the people behind her for a moment. "The Dark ones wish to hear you out, learn of your plans…"

I tense up, trying to understand the meaning of her words.

"And, if your plans are good, we will help you take him down."

I stand my ground, trying to push down the warmth filling my chest. How they convinced Arkadia, of all people, to hear me out was a complete mystery. Is this a trick? Had she listened to her followers and decided to go with their wants instead of her own fears?

"Are you suggesting that you would help us fight Lucifer?" I ask coolly, keeping my voice steady to hide the excitement. The people behind her freeze at the sound of my voice, their varied expressions on me.

She nods her head slowly, the fierce expression still there. I scan the crowd behind her, my breath quickening with every second. Most of the people before me are young, growing up inside a hidden sanctuary, unallowed to even play fight. It would take a miracle for them to last two seconds against Lucifer's army.

Time is on our side, however. Lucifer has called his army home, unable to suffer any more losses. He is clever and likely already making plans to build them back up quietly. *But how long can we afford to let him do that?* I ask myself. I have no idea how long it will take to train a band of shapeshifters. Would it be worth it in the end? *It has to be.*

I take a few steps toward her, letting my excitement become determination. I start to speak, letting the words out as they come into my head.

"The plan was to drive Lucifer's minions back into hiding, which we succeeded in, with only three of us. Now, we have a new task. Lucifer is hiding, and we have a chance to prepare ourselves to end his terror once and for all," The people around me straighten up slightly, leaning in to soak in every word. "We need to prepare ourselves. Train every able body that is willing to fight. We will go after him when ready, but we do not have a second to waste."

"So, you are suggesting that we train?" Arkadia asks.

"Yes, anyone with combat experience can help train those who do not. I can turn into a dragon, which is the form that Lucifer's minions fight in. That way, you can learn how to fight them." I turn my attention toward Orion, gesturing to him with an open hand. "He has experience fighting dragons, and he cannot fly. If Midnight and I could train him against the dragons, we can surely train all of you."

"And what if Lucifer doesn't show himself in open combat again?" Arkadia asks once more.

Midnight steps forward before I can say another word. "You have seen the prophecy as I have, Arkadia. Angel kills him. So, he will surely meet us again," She says confidently. *She has seen it...does that mean I can?* The thought comes into mind. I want to see it if there is genuinely a prophecy of me killing him.

"But what about them?" Arkadia gestures to the crowd. "They may be able to fight his minions, but Angel herself fought him and failed. How can we trust that she will be successful this time?" Anger rises in my chest.

"I didn't have you. Alone, I am no match for Lucifer and his army. But, with you all by my side, I am a sure match for Lucifer as you are a match for his army. I am not asking any of you to fight Lucifer himself; how can I? That is not your problem. You only need to deal with his minions so that I can have him for myself." I explain, hoping to give them some comfort.

"How do we know he won't control your mind again?" *I don't.*

"I am much stronger than I was then. And he controlled it with his minions' help, all at once. He will not be able to by himself." I let the words come out, hoping they are true. Arkadia seems to like that reply, her expression softening some. She brings her hands together, turning to face the people behind her.

"We have a lot to think about. Go home, think it over, and we will have an open meeting first thing tomorrow morning."

With her words, the crowd erupts into conversation, excited as they walk to their homes. If all goes well, this same crowd of eager people would be putting their own lives and their children at risk. I take a deep breath, turning back toward Midnight and Orion.

"Now what?"

"Let's have Orion show Boreas and his family to a hut. We need to talk." Midnight says, tilting her head toward our small group of griffins. *I hope I did the right thing taking them here.* I think to myself, giving him an encouraging smile before they head off after Orion.

I cautiously follow Midnight, unsure of what kind of "talk" she would want to have. My mind went to when she told me she had something to say, and we got distracted. *There are more important things happening right now.* I remind myself. No matter what it is, we must plan for what we will do moving forward.

Her hut is exactly how we left it the first time we were here, with nothing out of place. She said it is likely that mine is the same way. Arkadia may be stubborn, but she cares deeply for Midnight.

"Tomorrow morning, they will likely choose to have you stay here and train those willing. Arkadia will not like this, but I think she will come around. She loves her people, but she hates Lucifer more." Midnight starts confidently.

"I hope so. I would rather not risk the chance of Lucifer controlling my mind again." I say. The darkness, or whatever it is, is already strong enough as it is. The thought of Lucifer adding to it is absolutely terrifying…if this darkness is even from him.

"There won't be a chance of that. As you said, you're much stronger now. I am sure he will be able to feel it just as much as we can. It might scare him, giving us the edge we need." *Lucifer? Scared?* There is no way those two words go together.

I stay silent momentarily, unsure how to talk with her. It is clear that she has something to say; she has for months, but Midnight is not the best when it comes to opening up about things.

She clears her throat before continuing. "You know, that dark feeling you have…that you give off …it has gotten a lot stronger than before. I was actually kind of…” She trails off, concern lingering in her voice.

“Afraid the Sanctuary wasn’t going to let me in?” I finish her sentence with a sigh. She immediately lowers her gaze, nodding her head slightly. “Me too. I didn’t think I deserved to be here the first time, let alone now.” I continue. It had to be a good sign, though. Despite the evil desires inside of me begging for kills, I am still…me.

“I’m sorry, it was such a sudden fear once I realized you hadn’t come through yet. I saw your hesitation. You can tell me, what you’re feeling, you know. We can figure this out together.”

Figure this out together. I don’t know how well Midnight will handle learning that the darkness has a voice, let alone that I believe the dream was real. *What a silly concept.* Yet, every day it seems to be more and more likely.

What would Midnight think? She has seen the prophecy herself; perhaps it indicates this. *Unless it wasn’t part of the plan, but there is no way I can get out of a prophecy, right?*

“I feel like me, but…different. I can’t really explain it.” I tell her. “I wish I could show it to you…wait a minute…” I turn around, starting to pace the room. My mind shifts back to the dream, how Cobra somehow looked inside my mind, into my memories. *Can Midnight do that?*

Midnight tilts her head, watching me curiously. “What are you thinking, Angel?”

“It might not work, but what if I show you how I am feeling…or the memory I have. I could let you in completely and open my mind to you. Try and show you the memory…”

“The memory of what?”

“The dream.”

Chapter Twenty-Six

The "Dream"

Midnight doesn't say a word for several minutes after we successfully review my memory of the dream together. I opened my mind to her, concentrating my thoughts on when I was supposedly in the "World Of Chaos." It took us several attempts, as she had never tried something like this before. In fact, she claims no one has, at least not that she has heard of.

But sure enough, Midnight could watch the scenes through my eyes as if she was in a movie theatre. She even tensed up at parts, swearing she could feel my pain when Lana and I had our little spar. The hardest part was keeping our contact strong throughout the process, as any random thought I had would disrupt our contact with the memory.

Rewatching the dream, I came to the same conclusion that I am sure Midnight did: Cobra implanted a piece of his darkness in me and told me to let it strengthen me. I was in that strange place, my soul wholly intact and in an entirely different world while my body lay completely still in Lucifer's safehouse.

"Long ago, there were several prophesies made about you. I only saw one, which clearly stated that you would be the one to kill Lucifer," Midnight breaks the silence, her voice a low whisper. "If I remember right, there was a carving toward the end. It was of a man surrounded by these weird black spikes. I had no idea what it meant; no one did. I thought it was accidentally placed there from a different prophecy or just a random carving of some kind."

"You mean, that picture…it could have been of Cobra? That dream, it had been prophesized about?" I whisper, shock filling my voice. *I need to see this prophecy for myself.*

"It makes the most sense. Now, listen to me, Angel." She changes her focus, noticing the quickening of my breath. I meet her gaze, trying to keep the fear from showing. *I have that darkness in me…I have a piece of Cobra in me…* I let out a shudder.

The pieces are slowly starting to come together in my head. Even in my dream, I could feel how strong and deadly the darkness within Cobra could be. It terrified me. It caused him so much pain and anguish to even use it. It is clear now: it feeds off pain…off death.

Every time I kill one of Lucifer's minions, it fills me with joy. It is feeding off of me, off of their lives. *He still managed to control it.* I try to assure myself. He only gave me a small piece, after all.

"Angel," Midnight comes closer, placing a paw on my shoulder. "When they question the feeling you give off, just keep telling them it's a side effect of being controlled by Lucifer. This does not have to leave this room."

"It doesn't have to leave this room? Midnight, it is a part of me. It goes where I go. Why did he do this? I don't understand." I stammer, my composure slowly crumbling away. She hushes me quickly, gesturing toward the thin animal pelt door. I shake my head slightly before taking a deep breath, meeting her worried gaze.

"I promise you; it will be okay. If it was part of the prophecy, it was meant to happen. Maybe that's the true thing you need to be able to defeat Lucifer. Embrace this, Angel. Just keep it quiet for now, okay?" She whispers, bringing her face close to mine.

I look into her eyes, clinging to the confidence she has. *This was meant to happen.*

"Okay," I whisper, taking another deep breath. "We need to prepare ourselves for tomorrow." I change the subject, wanting nothing more than to discuss anything else.

We spend the rest of our day going over different scenarios of questions that might come up. Midnight makes it clear that this is an open meeting, so all of the Sanctuary can ask us questions as they please. Although they are won over for the most part, we need to look as professional as possible in answering them.

Arkadia will likely have a whole list of rebuttals, which I will do my best to keep my cool on. The last thing we need is a repeat of our first meeting. Without them, there is almost no chance of us successfully beating Lucifer.

We develop a basic training plan, which will require the help of both Boreas and Orion. It involves getting a few different teachers, all of whom will have a certain number of students per day. This way, we can focus on individual shapeshifters without being overwhelmed with too many. This will also allow them not to get overworked, as this will be a process.

Once we have enough shapeshifters in training and they all pass "performance" tests, we will coordinate how to draw Lucifer out of hiding. Midnight figures that once we go out in the open, he will gladly show himself, as it will be a good chance for him to wipe out the shapeshifters for good, or so he will think.

The only problem, however, is the timeline. We need time to train the shapeshifters to fight, but we don't want to give him enough time to rebuild his army. The fewer the dragons, the better. This is where having multiple teachers comes in, taking advantage of the time we have.

Arkadia starts the meeting the following day by allowing Midnight and me to present our detailed plan to the community, laying everything we have on the line. Once we finish, she opens the floor for anyone with questions.

"What about the young children? Surely you are not asking them to go into battle?" A woman asks, with her toddler son clinging to her side.

"Of course not. The only ones that will train are those that want to. If anyone under eighteen wants to, they will need their parent's permission." I answer calmly. She seems to like that, giving a gentle nod before sitting back down. *So far, so good.* I think to myself, looking around at the semi-happy faces.

Another person stands up, his stern eyes on me. "How are we supposed to train to fight against the dragons with shapeshifters that can't fly?" A few people nod in agreement, fear lingering in their eyes.

"Midnight and Orion both have killed minions. There are ways other than flying to take advantage of a dragon. They will both be your teachers." I gesture toward them, followed by a soft smile from Orion.

"It is true. I turn into a wolf and have managed to slay a few of the minions we came across."

"But you had a dragon by your side! Surely you practiced on her." Another woman exclaims, pointing her hand toward me.

"He did, and so will you. Anyone willing to fight can spar with me in dragon form." I reply calmly. *Didn't I already make this clear? Oh, well.* This answer satisfies them enough, as the crowd becomes quiet once more.

I shift my gaze toward Arkadia, sitting atop her chair, resting her elbow on her knee as she listens carefully. The fierceness in her expression is no longer there, just a blank stare as she listens to her people.

"How do we know Lucifer won't return before we are ready?"

"He is too busy rebuilding his army. He retreated when just the three of us were attacking his minions. He doesn't have much left." Midnight replies.

"How long can we afford to let him rebuild?" Another person chimes in.

"As long as we need. But, if we are going to train, we need to start immediately." Midnight continues, adding urgency to her voice. "If we do nothing, we will be stuck hiding forever, and surely he will find us once he has full control of the Earth."

The crowd did not like that.

There is an eruption of voices, each person trying to talk over the other. Within a few seconds, shouting broke out as people tried to be heard. It is hard to make out most of it, but some phrases were "act now" and "what are we waiting for?".

Within a few moments, the crowd turns their attention to Arkadia, shouting their thoughts toward her. They are done waiting, as most of them seem rather angry. She doesn't say a word, sitting calmly with her eyes closed.

After a few moments, she takes a deep breath and stands up, her eyes meeting mine. I freeze on the spot, not moving a muscle as she slowly moves through the crowd and approaches me. *This can't be good.* I think to myself, noting how quickly the shouting turned to silence. She stops a few feet in front of me, taking another deep breath before meeting my gaze.

"Looks like they are passionate about this," She starts, her voice the only sound heard. "You are all free to stay, and we will start planning where the training will take place. The meeting is dismissed." With her words, a few people break out into cheers.

"It's best we go." Midnight nudges me in my side, hoping to get out of there before they get too rowdy. I follow behind her, with Orion close behind. We stay silent as we exit, slipping away from the happy chaos within the hut.

Knowing that we had successfully gotten Arkadia on our side feels almost surreal. A new sense of hope fills me as we walk. For the first time in a long time, the thought of being able to kill the devil doesn't seem so impossible.

"I wish Justin were here. He would love this." I say as we make our way toward Midnight's hut. Only then would this day be truly perfect. Midnight flinches slightly at the sound of his name, nodding in agreement.

She had been the person to carry him away from that place, away from his deathbed. I can't even imagine how it must have felt to carry his corpse on her back. I don't think I would have been able to do it. *Where did she bury him? Did she even bury him?* I question myself. *Of course, she did. This is not the time.*

"We have a lot of preparations to do. Orion, can you handle talking with Boreas about being a teacher? He seems like a good man for the job." Midnight gets straight to business.

"Yes, it would be my pleasure." He replies happily.

"Good. Now, let's get to work."

Chapter Twenty-Seven

Preparations

We spent the entirety of the following week reorganizing the Sanctuary and preparing it for a training setup. The first step was to figure out who could help us teach the others to fight. So, we created a small council of teachers who will take turns training a set number of students. Arkadia also offered to let us use the field behind her hut as a training area, which is a good fit. It is the largest open spot within the barrier, about the size of a football field.

Midnight is in charge of scheduling and managing the recruits, which is a somewhat overwhelming task as a few more faces ask to join daily…not that it is a bad thing. It just makes me glad that Midnight is experienced enough to handle it.

I learned that there are fifty shapeshifters within the Sanctuary, apart from Midnight, Orion, and me. About a quarter of that number are children under eighteen, so we are still determining if they will join us in training. Midnight guesses that at least twenty will be willing to help us, although I would be happy with just one. Any number of fighters increases our chances, especially considering how the first battle went. Still, the thought of having that many people by my side when I must have Lucifer again feels pretty good. I just hope I don't let them down again.

Now that we are officially making good progress, I decided it was time for me to visit Justin's grave. The pain is there, but I can handle it now. With everything going well, it only makes sense for me to visit him. I never truly got to say my goodbye, after all. The only person with that knowledge is Midnight. Recently, when she isn't busy talking with the other shapeshifters, she has spent her free time locked up in her hut. I don't blame her, as now it is hard for us to walk freely without being asked a million questions.

I am in the middle of approaching her hut when Boreas comes up from behind me.

"Angel!" He calls, making me stop in my tracks. *So close.* I think to myself, looking longingly toward her hut. I turn to meet his gaze with a smile, trying to be polite. He has only been here for a week, and his glow radiates. He looks more cheerful than usual, with some papers in his hands. *What are you planning?* I question, having a feeling he is about to suggest something.

"Hey, I have been looking for you," he says as he reaches me, holding the papers out to me. "Midnight and I made up a schedule for the first week of training. I was hoping you could review it and see if it works for you?" *I can wait a little longer.* I say to myself, accepting the papers. They have a written plan for seven students, each with their own training times.

"You want me to do…pretests?" I ask him, noticing my name written next to each "pretest" time.

"Oh, yes. Just a little spar with each student in your dragon form. That way, we can keep a record of their progress. It will be a good way for you to get to know them individually, too." He says rather excitedly. *Get to know them individually.* I repeat to myself. The thought of making personal relationships with new shapeshifters sounds fantastic, apart from what comes after. *We must train them well.* There is no way I can bear the thought of having some of them perish.

"Sounds good. You might just have to remind me when I must do them," I say, handing it back to him and turning away.

"Wait! Did you notice the first one? It would be good for you and Orion to demonstrate for everyone. They are very eager."

My eyes linger on Midnight's hut. "Right now?"

"If that works for you, yes." His voice softens slightly. "But if you're busy…" He trails off, seeming to notice my distraction.

I turn myself toward him. "No, no, it can wait. Let's go." I reply.

I have been pushing it off for this long.

It only takes us a few minutes to reach the field, which is surrounded by a few onlookers whose faces light up as they notice us. I raise an eyebrow at Boreas, who simply waves me off and approaches the crowd with a warm smile.

"I got her! Now, please pay attention, all of you. You might learn something." His cheerful voice carries across the field.

I slowly walk into the center, surprised to see Orion waiting patiently. He meets me with a challenging stare, a smile playing on his lips. I scan the crowd around us, all of whom are staring rather eagerly. *How long has he been planning this?*

"I have never put on a show before, but don't be alarmed when I shift, those of you who have never seen a dragon," I say, raising my wings above my head. I lower my voice. "Are you ready to get embarrassed?"

Orion shakes his head and turns around, running around the field. *What is he up to?*

After one lap of him running and raising his arms with the shapeshifter's whoops and hollers, he jumps into the air to shift into his wolf form. He lands softly, continuing to run around once more. I stand my ground as he runs at me at full speed, his eyes focusing just above me. *Someone is a show-off.* He narrows his eyes as he approaches me, preparing himself to jump. I spread my wings out of the way as he takes off, jumping over my head, right between them.

"Impressive." I tease, feeding off the crowd's energy. Orion stays still, staring at me patiently as the crowd goes silent. "Oh, is it my turn?" I smile, not hesitating to leap into the air.

My heart pounds hard as I put on an aerial show, twisting and diving around for a couple of laps around Orion. I stop to hover above him, meeting the crowd with a wide smile. I notice Midnight approaching out of the corner of my eye, her curious eyes on us. *I should show her how much of a symbol I can be.* I think to myself, a light filling me that I have never felt before, pure excitement and joy, begging me to keep putting on a show for them. Anything to make Midnight proud. *If it's a showoff Orion wants, it's a showoff he's gonna get.* I smile, staring down at the excited crowd. *They seem to be enjoying it.*

Wanting to give them a little more, I jolt myself upward away from the crowd. I go into a dive, aiming straight for Orion. As I go, I shift into my dragon form, making cheers and gasps escape the other shifters as I get closer. I let out a triumphant roar as I level myself out, circling just above the field. I land hard directly in front of Orion, curling my lips into a mischievous smile. He takes a deep breath before dipping his head toward me. *That may have been a bit much.* I think to myself, feeling the nervousness coming off him now.

"Are you ready?" I ask him, lowering myself some. He does the same, meeting my gaze with determination. We slowly start circling each other, waiting for the other to strike first. We have done this many times along our journey across the country. He is more skilled than he was; the experience of fighting minions helped him immensely.

I lunge at him first, slamming into the ground just inches from him as he lunges away. As I turn, he jumps toward me, landing softly on my back. The crowd lets out soft gasps, surprised at his speed.

His triumph is short-lived as I let my body roll, making him jump off before my weight crushes him. I flick my tail at him as he runs off, causing him to trip slightly. He quickly recovers, pouncing at me once more. I give my wings a hard flick to stop him from going for my side, only to realize he went underneath.

He bites hard on my back leg, pulling me with all his strength. It causes me to fall on my side, losing my balance. He immediately let go, jumping onto my side as I try to get back on my feet. He scrambles around me, biting and clawing at my scales as fast as he can, carefully avoiding my wings. *Even in battle, he is so considerate—time to get rid of that.*

I reach around with my neck, trying desperately to grab ahold of him. He is almost as fast as Midnight, pestering me and moving around my body. As he tries to come toward my head, I clamp onto the scruff of his neck, tossing him to the side with a flick.

"You're getting faster," I state, watching as he returns to his feet, taking quick breaths. I give him a moment to recover, turning my attention to the crowd. "You'll notice that he avoided my wings, trying to go for my head. Against a real minion, you will want to go for the wings. Get rid of their flying ability so fighting them will be easier." I say to them, my attention turning back to Orion.

He comes at me once more, determination still strong in him. I swipe my tail toward him, but he jumps over it just in time. He doesn't falter, leaping toward me once more.

We go at this for about thirty minutes, leaping around and exerting most of our energy. As we go, our clumsiness increases more and more. I managed to trip him with my tail a second time, followed by holding him still with one of my talons.

"Do you surrender?" I pant, gently taking my foot off him. He groans, slowly standing up once more.

"If I weren't so exhausted, I would keep going." He replies, catching his breath.

"Angel wins!" Boreas exclaims happily, making his way over to us. "Though, I have to hand it to you, Orion. You managed to make her bleed!" He points toward the ground, a few blood splatters littering it. I turn to give Orion a proud look, noticing his wide-eyed stare at the ground.

"I'm sorry, I didn't realize I could do that…" He says slowly.

"Why are you apologizing? I just kicked your butt!" I laugh, shifting back into my human form. "Besides, do you see any scars?" I hold up my arms, gesturing to my untouched skin. The only blemish was a patch of dried blood lingering on my leg. Still, it was impressive that he managed to do minor damage. Warmth fills me at the thought of his improvement, knowing he might have a chance to fight against Lucifer's army.

Orion doesn't seem too amused by this, continuing to look at the blood stains. "Oh, relax," I say, approaching him for a hug. He tenses up at first but quickly gives in to my embrace. "We are still friends, don't worry so much. In fact, you should be proud of yourself for hurting the 'chosen one.'" I whisper to him before letting go.

"Thank you." He replies quietly. I gently smile, patting his back as we focus on the crowd. They are all staring at us with hopeful eyes as if waiting for us to say something.

"An actual minion will be easier to fight than me; I can promise you all that. Although it may not look like it, Orion did very well." I say, giving Orion another proud smile.

Within a few moments, Boreas makes his way back into the open field with a rather proud look on his face. He seemed pleased with the show we had just put on.

"Thank you, both. You are an inspiration to us all. I look forward to growing our partnership. Now, Angel, you may go. Do whatever it is I interrupted earlier. Orion and I can finish up here." He says, giving me a subtle wink. I breathe a sigh of relief before smiling at the people and walking off.

'*Can we talk?*' I reach out to Midnight as I walk. Her presence enters my mind in an instant.

'*Of course.*'

Chapter Twenty-Eight

Prophecy

"Is it the darkness again?" Midnight asks once we are inside her hut.

"No, I have gotten rather good at ignoring that," I reply, feeling discouraged that she would think this would be about the darkness.

"Oh, good." She replies softly. "I was worried that the fighting might have sparked something." *Sparked something?* Part of me is starting to regret telling her anything.

"It's not an important thing. I just came to ask where you buried Justin."

If Midnight had been in the middle of drinking something, she surely would have spit it out right then and there. Her eyes widen at my words, and I feel something come off her that I never had before, anxiety.

"You did bury him, right?" I question, fighting the lump in my throat. "You sent Orion away; surely you did not leave his corpse to rot?"

"You…shouldn't go see him. Not with everything we are working on. It could hinder our progress." I flare my nostrils at her, anger rising within me. The good feeling I had mere minutes ago quickly simmered out. *How is she going to not allow me to see his grave?*

"I can't try and find Maggie in fear of her being in danger. I don't know if my siblings are alive and can't search for them, and now I can't even go see Justin's grave?" I challenge, trying to make her see just how important this is.

"No." She replies sternly, trying to hide the fear coming off her. "We have more important things going on. Like what you did today with Orion, couldn't you feel the energy from everyone? You filled them with excitement and hope. I need you to keep this mindset you have, staying positive for them." I take a deep breath, trying to calm the anger within me. *Stop trying to change the subject. It's a simple request.* I think to myself, determined to get my answer.

"I can handle it. Where did you bury him?" I repeat, my eyes meeting hers. She stays silent, meeting my gaze with a fire of her own. Years ago, I would have cowered at her cold stare, but that little girl is long gone. "If you don't tell me, I will just do it myself. Who knows how long it will take, either?" I add, making her eye twitch slightly.

She breaks eye contact and turns away, pacing around the hut. *Why is it so hard for you to tell me where he is?* I question myself, feeling the anger continue to rise within me. The darkness also seems to enjoy this, filling me with dangerous thoughts. *No.* I think as sternly as possible within my head, pushing it down. I know Midnight is stubborn, but this feels ridiculous. She should trust me by now, knowing how much I have healed.

"Have you lost faith in me? You think I can't handle seeing his grave, yet I have already grieved. I just want to formally say goodbye. I shouldn't have to fight you for this…unless something else is going on? Does it have to do with what you wanted to talk to me about before?"

She stops in her tracks, turning to face me with one quick twist of her body. "I have never lost faith in you."

"Then why won't you tell me where you buried him? Why Midnight?" I raise my voice, starting to plead. "He was my best friend!"

"I didn't bury him, okay!" She blurts out, letting her ears go flat. I take a few steps back from her, letting her words sink in. "He didn't need to be buried… but I swear, he is safe. It was best for him…best for you…best for the task you must do still, and the prophecy—"

"He. Is. Safe." I repeat slowly, letting her words sink in. "He didn't need to be buried. Are you suggesting what I think you are?" I ask her, feeling the darkness building on my rage.

"Yes."

"Wait," I stammer, trying to simmer my fury. "Are you telling me that he has been *alive* this entire time? I don't understand…" I clench my fists into balls, pacing the floor in front of her. The darkness is swirling within me now, begging to come out. *There is no way... It can't be true. She wouldn't lie to me like this.*

Midnight's eyes lower to the ground, and her paw softly digs at the floor in front of her, her eyes full of regret.

"Angel, I–"

"Don't. Don't try to make it better. How could you? I mean, how *could* you? You saw what I was. The amount of torture I have put myself through. Now that I am finally okay with it, you are coming to me with this?" I huff, tears swelling in my eyes. "He's ALIVE! Midnight. Alive. Breathing. You knew it and let both of us think the other was dead!" I shout at her. Midnight's ears go back for a moment, a rage of her own building up. Her eyes lift to meet mine, only to be filled with shock.

"Your wings…the darkness…"

"My wings? That's what you're concerned about?" I snap, letting out a loud breath before stretching them to my sides. My heart drops momentarily as I notice; they are entirely black. "Yeah, that's a perk of being filled with darkness; my anger tends to show." I couldn't care less if anyone saw me at this point.

"I'm sorry, I thought it was for the best. He is safe, Angel. They both are. They're not safe with you; Lucifer is still–"

"Where are they?" I cut her off.

"Safe."

"Midnight, if you ever want a chance at fixing our relationship, you need to tell me. If I have to find him on my own, which I will, I will never speak to you again." She takes a step back, looking at me with complete horror.

"Europe, near Bosnia." I give her a tiny nod before spinning toward the door. It looks like I will finally be traveling to another country.

I shove myself through the pelt, not caring as it falls to the ground. A few people gather outside, likely drawn in by our shouting. Their faces drain of color at the sight of my black wings. Orion takes a few steps forward, his eyes filled with concern. I raise a hand at him, turning my attention toward the sky. Nothing matters at this moment; I just have to get to him. I jump with all my strength, shooting into the air like a bullet as the ground around me shakes.

My heart races as I fly, my rage at Midnight giving me more

speed and endurance than I thought possible. I move effortlessly over the vast ocean, flying faster than ever. *This darkness does have some perks.*

* * *

"This has to be it," Justin whispers, his eyes lingering on the stone wall before him. It is almost impossible to see deep within the rainforest, despite its large appearance. It is completely covered in various branches and flowing vines. He gently places a hand on the front, wiping away layers of dust and dirt. A faint carving stands out, a sword. He takes a deep breath and gently traces it with his finger. The same sword changed his life, giving him a strength that should be impossible; the same one that led Angel to her death.

"That's the sword, isn't it?" Maggie whispers, placing a hand on his shoulder. "We finally found something!" She chirps, pulling her son around for a warm embrace. He lets out a slight squeal through his wide smile. After years of searching, they had *finally* found something.

"Now, according to this," he carefully eyes the old scroll, "I just have to place my hand firmly on it and say 'open.' If I am confident, it should do as I say."

"That seems too easy; haven't you watched the movies? There's always something." Maggie replies, taking a small step backward as he firmly presses his hand on the stone. He rolls his eyes. He loves his mother, but she sure is overly cautious.

"They're movies. This is reality." He takes a deep breath. "This is for you," he whispers before turning his focus back toward the stone. "Open." A tiny flicker of green flashes from his palm and into the stone sword, making a low rumbling sound as the stone opens inward. *I can't believe that worked.* He thinks to himself, staring excitedly into the new opening. Maggie takes a few more steps back. "So much for the shapeshifters being the only ones allowed in." He says, annoyance in his voice. *What else is Midnight lying about?* He lets the thought come into mind.

"I don't know Justin…" Maggie says worriedly, staring into the dark abyss. "This doesn't seem safe." He takes a step into it, slowly turning back toward her.

"If we don't go in, what was the point of these past few years, mom? I have to do this. If I don't… it'll feel pointless, and the hope will be all gone. And I must see it for–" Maggie cuts him off, abruptly grabbing his hand.

"You're right. We have to, for Angel," She says calmly, turning her attention toward the cave in front of them. It is completely black, the light from the opening only covering the mouth of it. They take a few more steps in, the door instantly shutting behind them. Maggie shivers before taking a deep breath. "This is fine."

Justin squeezes her hand before letting go, holding his arms out in front of himself as he walks. Without the light from the entrance, it is pitch black. Maggie grabs the back of his shirt, carefully following close behind him. The ground is surprisingly smooth, reminding him of Midnight's old cave…oh how he longed to see it again. He wanted nothing more than to be home, even though he was still upset with her. He knows he can never go back there now, not with all the dragons freely roaming. He is powerless without the sword bonded to him.

A 'whoosh' fills the cave as a harsh breeze flows through, lighting the torches on the walls with a green flame.

"Where did that even come from?" Maggie gasps, looking wildly around them.

The cave is even bigger than they thought. The walls stretch out on either side of them, going on for about a hundred feet. The cave's floor is as smooth as concrete and black as night.

"Wow, it looks like obsidian." Justin comments, running his hand along the wall as he leads the way. Maggie follows closely behind him, her eyes darting every which way. She does not like anything about this at all. *Please don't be any bats.* She thinks to herself.

Near the back side of the cave, an old looking stone ruin lays on a large pedestal, lit by the dancing green flames nearby. All of Justin's searching was for this moment; nothing else matters now.

On top of the pedestal is a series of carved stones laid in a perfect line. They make their way to the far left of them, noticing a carving of a baby with wings attached to its back. He eagerly walks along the ruin, staring intently at each one.

"Is this… the prophecy?" Maggie asks, staring in awe at the following picture, a cat with wings.

"Yes, the one Midnight told me about." He replies, continuing to follow the carvings. The next one was a young boy holding the sword over a dead dragon. *My first kill.* He thought to himself. "And to think, she told me that only shapeshifters can come here."

"Wait… Midnight knew you would help Angel?" Maggie asks, surprised to see the carving that resembles her son. "I wonder how they made these…" She pauses, her eyes widening at the next one. Angel is kneeling, staring at a lifeless body in front of her.

"Oh my…" Maggie staggers backward. "Midnight saw this prophecy, and she didn't—"

"Look," Justin cuts her off, pointing to the next one. Angel is standing in front of a large, masked figure with many spike-like arms reaching into her. "Do you think this means—" Justin chokes on his words "that she could be…alive?" He lets himself fall to his knees as his body starts to shake.

"I don't know. I mean, who is that man there? It looks like he is killing her. But if so… that's after when she stabbed herself…"

"So, there's a chance, mom!" He jumps back up, frantically looking at the pedestal for more pieces, only to find two holes in the end, the carvings completely smashed. "I don't get it; why would someone destroy it?" He balls his hands into fists, the small amount of hope seeping away. "We need to find Midnight. She has so much explaining to do."

"Right. Let me take some pictures real quick." Maggie says quietly, trying to fight off the rage building in her. If she had known her son was in a prophecy to be killed, there is no way she would have let Midnight train him.

Justin turns around, letting his eyes meet the floor for a moment. He takes a step, only to stop abruptly in his tracks. A warm flicker reaches his mind, tapping lightly on his walls; Angel had done well at teaching him how to keep people out. He shakes his head to fend it off, raising his eyes to the dimly lit area around them.

"Someone is near." He warns, the warm feeling suddenly cracking at his walls again with much more force. Justin takes a step backward; the person trying to reach him is *desperate.* Yet, something inside him wanted to drop his guard so it could enter. "They're trying to reach my mind, but it's weird… It seems good."

"Maybe it's Midnight?" Maggie shrugs her shoulders, coming up beside him. He shakes his head.

"No," The person tries again, the warm sensation cracking his walls for a moment, making him drop into a kneel. It fills him with comfort, grief, anger, and love.

"Justin?" Maggie grabs his shoulders, giving him a gentle shake. He is almost unaware, for his heart starts to leap out of his chest. That feeling was all too familiar. The person reaching him was clearly broken, but they knew him. It was *her*.

'Justin!' Angel's voice booms inside his mind, filling him with hope. He starts to sob into his mother's shoulder, shaking uncontrollably as she frantically tries to figure out what is wrong. He lets his barrier tumble, reaching out and grabbing onto Angel's warmth in his head. It shines bright, clinging onto his mind immediately. With a gasp, they connect as they had been years ago.

"Angel." He whispers.

Maggie perks up behind him, her eyes wide toward the still closed cave entrance. Justin slowly pushes her off, standing up. His hands tremble madly as he walks toward the stone, clinging to the feeling of her. It continues to grow, becoming stronger the closer she gets; she is moving at an incredible speed, relying on their connection to find him.

'I think I am here.' Her voice says ever so gently as a loud crash erupts outside the cave, making Maggie gasp. Justin breaks off into a run, moving as fast as his legs can carry him. He skids to a halt at the entrance, holding his breath as the stone rolls away. The air leaves his lungs as he notices her shaking off leaves and dirt from her beautiful cheetah self. She freezes instantly as they lock eyes, both standing entirely still. He holds in a gasp as he notices the blackness of her wings, littering the once pure white.

"Oh, Justin…" Angel says quietly, sorrow filling her voice. He immediately launches himself forward, wrapping his arms around her furry neck in a tight embrace as he falls onto his knees. The fur instantly disappears as she shifts, her soft arms now wrapping around him just a little too hard. "I'm so sorry." She cries, burying her face into his neck. The color means nothing; it's still her.

"Shh." he hushes her, running a hand through her messy hair. Her grip on him tightens even more, causing him to grunt softly. She instantly releases him, meeting his gaze with an embarrassed smile. His breath stops momentarily as he takes her in; she is no longer that young girl he remembered. Her face is much more defined and feminine, her lips full and quivering as her dazzling green eyes stare into his. He cups her cheeks gently in his hands, prompting her to close her eyes with a soft smile. At this moment, he is sure his heart could leap right out of his chest.

Something behind them moves, and Angel's eyes lock on what he figured to be his mom. Angel's wings stiffen as she straightens up at the sight of Maggie. She gently untangles herself from his embrace, guilt covering her face. *I killed her son...at least, I thought I did.* She thinks, making her gaze drop to the ground in front of Maggie.

"Don't try and hide those beautiful eyes from me, young lady." Maggie chokes, opening her arms toward Angel, gesturing for her to come. Angel doesn't hesitate now, running at her and nearly knocking her over as they make contact.

Justin's heart fills with warmth as he watches them hug. He knew Maggie never held a grudge against Angel—neither of them did. As far as he was concerned, it was all Lucifer. He wanted nothing more than to watch him burn. And with Angel back, the idea seemed more possible than ever.

Epilogue

Orion and Boreas head to the training grounds, preparing to start another class. The field behind Arkadia's hut has been serving them well. Midnight and Arkadia had been helping them run things, talking to all the young and old members who wanted to begin training. Some had no experience, while others just wanted a refresher, as it has been years since their last real fight.

With Angel gone, Arkadia put them in charge of the bulk of the training. It is their job to keep everyone's spirits high and hopeful that she will return sometime soon. This was a relatively easy task for Orion, as he does not doubt she would return. The hard part was proving to everyone that she was still good. Many of them had seen her when she stormed off with her pure black wings. He figured this would happen eventually, as it is hard to hide when you are inside an entire village of shapeshifters. He just hopes she is okay, wherever she is.

He could hardly believe Midnight had gone to such lengths to keep Justin safe, or so she called it. Angel has every right to be mad; he was too. She is his closest friend, so anyone hurting her also hurts him.

Although he was furious with Midnight, he was excellent at keeping it from her. Despite the wall she had put up, she was clearly distraught about Angel's quick departure. Everyone had heard her anger…and felt it. Midnight did not need any more guilt than she already had. Part of him thinks that is why Arkadia made Midnight in charge of organizing the training, to keep her mind off things. It seemed to be working well enough.

"There you are! You have three students waiting for their lesson." Midnight brings him out of his thoughts, being the pushy leader she is. Boreas scowls beside him, seeming rather annoyed at her impatience.

"We need to have breakfast before teaching," Boreas says just loud enough for her to hear, walking past without looking in her direction. Midnight flattens her ears but doesn't say a word. *Does he have to be so cold to her?* Orion tries not to wince.

As they make their way around the hut, three young men come into view, their faces lighting up at the sight of them.

The oldest-looking one gives Orion a happy smile. "I was hoping we would get you! We all shift into wolves, runs in the family."

Orion meets his smile with his own, glad to have some like kind to work with. He has been struggling with one of his other students, Laden, who turns into a giant serpent. He enjoys wrapping around him and Boreas, squeezing just a bit too tight during their exercises.

"Then it will be good for you to work with the both of us, as Boreas can teach you how to handle flying opponents." He says confidently, nodding in his direction. Boreas smiles before shifting into his griffin form, letting out a piercing screech.

The youngest of the boys jumps backward. "Wait, aren't you going to give us some pointers first?" His voice shakes. Orion shifts into his wolf form, prompting the three boys to do the same.

"We believe it is best to learn by experience. Consider this a pretest. Follow your instincts, and we will build on your strengths and weaknesses. What's your name?"

The youngest lowers his head slightly before speaking. "Apollo."

"Alright, Apollo, you're up first," Orion says, not waiting a moment to pounce. He has no time to waste.

After four hours have passed, Boreas and Orion dismiss their recruits. They spent the day taking turns sparring with the three of them, shouting out tips and pointers as they went. They did surprisingly well, letting their fight instincts kick in as they were attacked, at least when they went against Orion.

Boreas was a whole different story, as they struggled to find ways to combat him once he was in the air. Because of this, Boreas sent them away with homework. They are to run daily, as fast and long as they possibly can. This will allow them to build their speed and endurance, making them better at maneuvering around a flying target.

Arkadia still refuses to let the younger students outside the barrier to train, not wanting to risk exposure to stray minions lurking. This is understandable to Orion, as he would hate to have someone injured due to his order that they train. Then again, he will eventually send them into battle with Angel by their side.

"How were they?" Midnight asks as Orion walks out from the field.

"Decent, they are very good at trusting their instincts. But not so good dealing with flight."

"Sounds familiar." She tries to tease him.

"Hopefully, they can learn fast enough." He replies, keeping the seriousness. He can tolerate her, but being friendly is an entirely different challenge.

"They will. Lucifer is too busy rebuilding what we destroyed."

"Too busy creating more enemies that can hurt them." He replies coldly. Midnight lets out a sigh.

"They need time. Besides, the humans are hiding. It will be much harder for him to recruit them than before. Do not worry so much; fighting is in their blood." She tries to comfort him. He nods in agreement, hoping to put an end to the conversation.

They stay silent for a moment, awkwardly sitting as they examine the village before them. It is much different than the first time they were here; children are now free to shift, run around, and play fight as they please. Even the adults are in better moods, sparring freely in the open, laughing and shouting at one another. *At least everyone seems happier.* He smiles.

"Have you…felt anything?" Midnight breaks the silence, the guard in her voice replaced by worry.

"Felt anything?" He asks, trying to understand what she means. *Oh.* He realizes. "No, I have not." He answers before she can explain, a coldness rising within him. It had been a month since Angel's departure, and she had shut them both out completely. He understood why she would shut Midnight out…but why him? He didn't understand what he had done.

"I see. I hope she's okay, wherever she is." Midnight chokes, a tear sliding down her cheek. *She really is full of guilt.* Orion thinks to himself, unable to stop his arm from sliding around her fur. Midnight shudders in a moment of weakness, letting her tears fall freely. "I should have told them everything. Stupid prophesies." She chokes.

He stays silent while she sobs, trying his best to comfort her. Even though not telling them was the worst decision she could make, she still seemed rather torn up about it. *She had her reasons, and they were good enough for her.* He tells himself, the pity rising within him.

A rather familiar dark feeling suddenly hits him, filling him with hope rather than fear. He isn't the only one, as Midnight immediately perks up beside him, her attention focused on something in the distance.

The end...

For now.

In Case you're Curious

The Oath of the Sword

*This oath is meant to bond the user to the sword. In the event that their heart is not pure, the sword will reject this oath.

"I, insert name here, humbly swear to follow the oath of the sword. I recognize that this blade was crafted by God himself, and no one is worthy to possess it. I swear that I will only use this sword for its intended purpose: to kill evil shifters. I will not use this sword against anyone with a good heart or any human being regardless of their morality. Should I do so, the oath shall be broken.

I acknowledge that this weapon will empower me, giving me powers no human should possess. I will only use these powers against evil shifters, and never take advantage of them for personal gain.

I swear to use this sword to protect my shapeshifter, as I am now their guard. I will fight alongside them at all times, for the rest of my days. I will not harm my shapeshifter in any way, unless I have no other option. In the event that my shapeshifter becomes corrupt, I will end them, thus freeing me from this oath. If I fail to do so, the oath will be broken and all connection shall be lost.

I swear to be the best I can for my shapeshifter and acknowledge that God himself is allowing me to use such a powerful weapon. I pray that I am worthy, and only God himself may judge me.

Read an excerpt of

Angel: Armageddon

Coming soon

Shortcomings

I release my grip on Maggie, water clouding my vision as I take her in. *She must hate me.* I think to myself, meeting her gentle eyes once more. She cups my cheeks in her cracked hands, smiling as the tears flow freely. *How can you look me in the eyes and smile at the same time?* I swallow hard, wishing she would let me escape her gentle eyes.

"Whatever it is you are thinking, stop." She whispers, forcing me to keep eye contact. "We are all okay. Especially now that we know you're safe." I close my eyes, letting out a soft sigh as she moves one of her hands to my wing.

"We changed. But we are okay." She adds, a hint of concern lingering in her voice.

"I know… They aren't pure anymore. I… I am not pure anymore." I struggle to get the last part out. *How can she even look at me?* I question, tucking my wings in as much as I can.

Maggie gently grabs ahold of one, her gaze firmly meeting mine. "Don't try to hide. Let us see." She commands, taking a couple steps away from me.

I give her a discouraged nod, reluctantly spreading them out as far as I can. She eyes them carefully, muscles in her face twitching as she thinks. Justin stares from a distance, keeping quiet.

After a minute or two, she crosses her arms. "They are beautiful. I don't know why you would want to hide them." *Beautiful.* I repeat, disbelief in my voice.

"They aren't perfect anymore." I object.

"You know, Angel, sometimes, you have to crack something to make it glow. This change only shows your growth." She says softly. "You are perfectly…imperfect."

Her words make me think of something Midnight once said to me, and it sounded suspiciously similar. I give her a weak smile, turning my attention towards the dangerously quiet Justin.

He has a blank stare, completely lost in thought. After a few more seconds of silence, I tilt my head to try and get his attention. His glossed over eyes flicker as he comes back to reality.

"Sorry." He apologizes, his eyes looking towards the cave, then back to me. I tilt my head. "As much as I want to know why your wings are like that… I have to show you something first." He says, pointing his head back towards that cave. *And just like that, the reunion is over.* I think to myself, curiosity replacing the guilt within me.

Without a second word, he makes his way towards it. I glance at Maggie, whose expression has gone cold.

"Straight to the point." She complains under her breath. We follow Justin inside.

After taking one step within the cave, it becomes clear how unnatural it is. The floor is a perfectly smooth obsidian, sparkling green from the flames on the walls. *How on Earth did they find this place?* I question.

Justin leads up to the very back of the cave, which has an array of stone carvings. He takes a step onto the pedestal, pausing before turning himself around to face me. His eyes meet mine and he takes a deep breath.

"We found your prophecy, Angel. We had to see for ourselves. I just knew there had to be something Midnight wasn't telling us, and I was right." He says, extending his arms out to gesture towards the carvings around him. "You should take a close look." His voice shakes slightly, lingering anger rising within him.

I hesitantly step forward, keeping eye contact with him as I move past. "Is this the same one Midnight saw?" I question, turning my attention towards the first few panels.

Justin nods, placing his hand on the one closest to him. "She has a LOT to explain." His voice turns cold.

"I agree. She didn't tell me you have been alive this entire time." I say, making my way towards the one he is pointing at.

My heart sinks as soon as I see it. Me, on my knees, hunched over a lifeless body. *Justin's* lifeless body. I take a few steps back, clutching my chest as I gasp for air. *She knew. She KNEW.* I repeat to myself, feeling the darkness start to creep into my emotions. *Oh, please don't.* I protest.

'*You should kill her. She lied to you, more than once.*' It speaks, filling me with rage as I continue to step away from Maggie and Justin. My fists clench into tight balls as the darkness erupts within me.

"She lied," I hiss.

Maggie's eyes widen with fear and she promptly pushes Justin behind her. She holds her arms out, keeping him in place as she holds eye contact with me. Sensing their fear instantly snaps me back to reality, making me notice the pure blackness of my wings. *Oh. What have I done?*

I step back, taking staggering breaths as my anger rapidly turns to guilt. "I—I'm sorry…This is not how I wanted you to find out…" I trail off, letting my gaze meet the floor in defeat.

Justin pushes Maggie out of his way, watching me with open shock. "Is…is it still you?"

I close my eyes for a moment, letting the cool cave air fill my lungs. "Yes." I whisper.

"I have only ever seen your wings do that one other time… when you weren't you." He says, watching as my wings lighten back up. "This is different."

"They do that a lot now." I answer. "But I promise you," I meet Maggie's terrified gaze. "I have full control."

"How did you change so much? Surely Lucifer couldn't have done this much damage?" He questions, taking a step closer. Unable to meet his eyes, I glance around the cave. The final carving stands out like a sore thumb as soon as I notice it.

"Him," I point, unable to believe my eyes. "Cobra."

Justin and Maggie exchange looks as something connects within their minds.

"How could one person change you?" Justin asks.

"Well, Justin… after I killed you…or, after I thought I did," I correct myself. "I stabbed myself in the heart with the sword."

"You did die, didn't you?" Maggie questions, horror in her face.

"I honestly don't know. I woke up in an entirely differ-ent…world. And, long story short, I took a piece of it with me when I reconnected with this one."

Justin tilts his head, trying to make sense of it all.

How can I explain this in any way where it'll make sense? I think to myself, feeling the darkness within me.

'Can I make other people see you?' I ask it. Without a word, the darkness creeps out of my chest and up my arm, filling it with cold-ness.

I hold my hand in front of me, palm facing up. Within a few sec-onds, a black, smoke-like substance appears, creeping around my hand. *You aren't for the faint of heart.* I think to myself as I watch it.

Justin's eyes widen, and he turns back to the carving. "It is like the picture. That person…Cobra, you have his power? Did he already do what he did in this carving?" He asks, a hint of fear entering his voice.

"I don't know. When I was about to leave that world, he told me that I'll need it. That it would make me stronger."

"It looks evil." Maggie adds, her frightened expression lingering on her face.

"It is. But I am in control of it." I answer, blocking it off once more to make it disappear. I take a few steps towards her, placing a hand on my chest. "I promise you, Maggie, I am still me. You can ask my anything about it, and I'll be honest with you. I just ask that you trust me. Please." I plead to her, giving her the softest expression I can manage.

She takes a deep breath, her own face relaxing. "I still see you." She says gently, giving me a small smile. "But I do have a lot of ques-tions."

Acknowledgements

I am so thankful for everyone who has made this series possible. (Seriously, you guys are amazing). I never thought I would be able to get one book published, let alone two. This has been an incredible learning experience, and I cannot wait to see just how far Angel can fly.

About The Author

S. N. MONTOYA is the author of the ongoing Angel series. Born and raised in northern Michigan, she loves the outdoors and the creatures within them. When she is not writing, she plays video games, draws, rides horses, and splashes around in mermaid tails. You can find her on Instagram and Facebook @s.n.montoya, where she likes to share her writing progress and photos of her daily adventures. She resides in northern Michigan with her husband, Eric, several cats, and snakes.